Ra retired thousands of years ago, when he decided that would be safer for his pantheon and the human world. He still believes that, but a series of natural disasters pull him away from peace. He worries that his enemy is breaking out of the underworld, and if that happens, it will only mean one thing — war. Ra will do what he can to prevent that, and in the meantime, maybe it's time for him to see what he'll be saving.

Frey is a minor god in his pantheon, and he likes things that way. After exposing himself to Odin's wrath by helping save Loki, he moves to Finland, hoping to find peace. He does, but he also finds Ra, one of the most powerful gods of the Egyptian pantheon, wandering around.

Frey takes Ra under his wing, but they can't ignore what's happening outside their corner of the world even as they fall in love. Frey is having visions of a giant snake, and Ra knows exactly who it is. Together, they'll have to find Apophis's ally to stop the natural disasters, but even if they do, it'll only be the beginning of the fight.

Darkness Rising
Copyright © 2022 Catherine Lievens
ISBN: 978-1-4874-3710-7
Cover art by Angela Waters

Published by eXtasy Books Inc

Look for us online at:
www.eXtasybooks.com

Darkness Rising
For the Gods' Amusement 4

By

Catherine Lievens

CHAPTER ONE

Something was wrong with Ra. He didn't know what it was, but he didn't like it.

He walked down the hallway, knowing he should return to his wing of the palace but unable to do so. His wing had always been his safe place, the only place he could call home, but lately it had started to feel too small for him. That didn't make sense because he hadn't changed his body in any way, and he certainly hadn't grown it taller or wider, yet here he was, feeling as if the walls were closing in on him.

It was because of his parent. They'd pulled him into a fight against gods from another pantheon, and while Ra wasn't sure that was the best idea, he'd been unable to say no. He'd never been able to say no to Nu. They meant more to him than to most of the other gods in their pantheon, but then, they were his parent. They'd directly birthed Ra and his two brothers, while the other gods in the pantheon were more distant. Nu was their grandparent, great-grandparent, or something like that. Ra had lost count of the generations, and he was sure he wasn't the only one.

It was one of the things being an immortal god did to you.

But Ra had been content before. He'd stayed in his wing, had read, watched TV, and enjoyed being retired. He wanted to go back to that and ignore the world outside of the palace, but he couldn't find the peace he'd had before. He didn't understand why, but he was feeling restless, and something had to be done.

He needed help.

Ra usually disliked admitting he needed anything from anyone, let alone help, but he could always go to Nu. They'd be happy to see him and have words of advice he sorely needed. Maybe they'd be able to tell him why he felt so unsettled, as if something disastrous was about to happen.

Ra probably felt that way because he'd been watching too much human TV. Humans never had an easy life, but things seemed to have gotten worse lately with all the natural disasters. It wasn't any of Ra's business anymore, but he liked keeping up to date in some ways. He watched the human news, but that was all he was interested in. Humans were nothing to him, or at least, they'd been nothing until two of them had entered his family.

He still had no idea what to think of that.

He'd been wandering aimlessly down hallways in the palace, but now that he'd decided to visit Nu, he knew where to go. It felt good to have a purpose, and he strode down the next hallway with his back straighter and head held high. He crossed paths with a few minor gods, and all of them bowed and plastered their backs against the wall as he walked past them. It was kind of ridiculous, since they were family, but he didn't have time to stop and make small talk.

Although that might help him feel less bored.

But if there was something he disliked even more than humans, it was his immense family. They never got along and always bickered, fought, or tried to kill each other. That was one of the reasons Ra had retired, although not the main one. He always got stressed when he spent any length of time with his family, although lately, he'd been spending more time with Nu, which meant he'd also been spending more time with Sed and Qebui.

He wasn't sure what to think of them. They were his great-great-great-grandchildren or something like that. It was never easy to keep count with such a massive family tree, and Ra had stopped trying a long time ago. He liked them, though. They didn't take themselves as seriously as most of the other gods did, and they'd chosen human lovers. It was an odd choice, especially for a lengthy relationship, but it wasn't unheard of. Those who did that were usually at the fringe of the pantheon, though.

Ra supposed Qebui and Sed *were* at the fringe. They were minor gods, but he liked them more than he liked his own children. He wasn't about to tell anyone but Nu about that. It would start a war, and he had no intention of dealing with any of that.

He finally reached Nu's door and quickly knocked. It took his parent a moment to reach him, but when the door opened, they beamed.

"Did we have an appointment I forgot about?" they asked, waving Ra inside.

"No. I was wandering and decided to come to talk to you."

Their eyes sparkled. "It's good to hear you still need my opinion and advice, even though you're millennia old."

"I'll always need you. There's no one as smart and full of wisdom as you are."

"Flattery will get you anything," they commented as they led the way toward the terrace.

Ra moved to follow them, but he tripped over Nu's cat. The thing wound around Ra's ankles, and Ra glared at it. It didn't seem to care, though, following Ra outside once he started moving again.

Nu sat in one of the chairs around the long table where they often shared meals. Ra took one of the other chairs, while the cat jumped into Nu's lap. They stroked the cat's head, not seeming to care that it was mummified.

"So, to what do I owe this pleasure?" Nu asked.

"I'm worried."

"About what? Are you feeling lonely again?"

Ra glared. "I don't get lonely."

"Sure you don't. What are you worried about if it's not that?"

Ra tapped his fingertips onto the table. "Have you been following the human news?"

"I usually don't, but with Sed and Qebui being down there, I've started to. Are you talking about the earthquakes and storms?"

"Yes. I'm sure it's nothing, but I can't help but worry." Ra hesitated. He wouldn't tell this to anyone else, but he could be honest with Nu. "I feel like something big is going to happen, and soon. It's like the world is waiting and holding its breath in anticipation, and I don't feel like anything good can come out of that. It's probably just a coincidence and I need to stop watching the news, but I'm uneasy."

Ra had been convinced Nu would wave away his worries. That wasn't what happened, though. Instead, Nu slowly nodded.

"I feel the same," they admitted.

That wasn't what Ra had hoped to hear. "It's probably just a coincidence."

"Maybe, maybe not. I don't think there's any way for us to find out, at least at the moment. You probably shouldn't obsess over this."

"I'm not obsessing over anything."

Nu arched a brow. "Aren't you? Don't you know I have eyes and ears everywhere in this palace? I'm very much aware of the fact that you've been restless."

"That's because of you," Ra accused. "You brought me in for that thing with your friend, and I haven't been able to stop thinking about it."

A knowing smile curled Nu's lips. "You enjoyed being useful and want that back, but you can't have it as long as you stick to the sky palace."

"Why do you call it that? It's not the sky palace. It's just our palace." But Ra knew why Nu called it that. It was to make a difference between this palace and the one down in the human realm where Sed and Qebui lived.

"No matter what I call it, the problem is the same. You're lonely."

"How can I be lonely when I'm surrounded by people?"

"You don't need other gods. You need something more."

"I don't *need* anything. I'm self-sufficient, and I have been for decades."

"No one should spend most of their time alone. I think you should find love."

Ra's brain froze. *Love?* "It's been a long time since I had love."

"And that's why you should find it again. You're not going to be happy spending time with the other gods in our pantheon. There's a reason you're retired and stayed away from them until recently. I don't blame you. They can be tiresome, and their constant bickering gets on my nerves. I much prefer spending time with Qebui, Sed, and their partners. Maybe that's what you should do. You could go down to their palace and maybe meet a nice human."

"I can't be with a human." It would be a scandal and not something Ra wanted to deal with.

"With whom, then? Someone from our pantheon?"

Just the thought made Ra shudder in horror. "We're all related one way or another."

"That hasn't stopped most of them from finding love with each other. You did once, too."

Ra was already shaking his head. "No."

"Then someone with another pantheon?"

Ra could imagine that even less. "I don't need love. I don't need anyone or anything."

"Everyone does, even powerful gods. I'm not going to kick

you out of the sky palace. I just believe it would be beneficial to you to spend more time in the human realm. Visit your grandsons. Spend time with them, get to know their partners. Stay away from the sky palace until you feel better."

Maybe that was the answer. Ra couldn't help but wonder about the natural disasters, though. Spending time in the human world would help him find the cause behind them. Whether that cause was natural or godly, he wondered if there was anything he could do to stop them.

Frey glanced around his bedroom. He was here to pack, but he wasn't sure what to take with him. The house he'd acquired in the human world wasn't big, but he didn't need much. There was a reason he was leaving Asgard—many reasons, actually—and it was that he needed a change. Life in Asgard had grown heavy over the past few weeks, and he disliked it. He needed out. He couldn't wait to move and be on his own, but before that could happen, he had to grab his things and close off his palace in Asgard.

Easier said than done.

Frey had researched the country where he'd bought his new house, so he knew what to expect when it came to the weather. He could use his godly powers to make himself warm or cold, but he'd decided he wanted to try living as a human as much as possible. It would be ridiculous to most of the gods, but not to Frey.

He wanted as much distance as possible between himself and Asgard, and that included the gods who lived here and their powers. Frey would never be able to pass for human, especially since he was taking Gullinbursti with him. No human would see the giant boar and think he was normal. But he was Frey's pet, and Frey wasn't about to leave him behind.

Frey pushed a strand of long hair away from his face and

sighed. He needed to start somewhere, and soon. Someone was bound to realize what he was doing eventually, and he had no way to know what Odin's reaction would be. He'd rather not find out, at least not until he was as far away as possible from Asgard.

Something pushed against his leg, and he looked down to find Gul staring up at him. The boar could tell something was wrong, and Frey didn't want to worry him, so he gave a good scratch between Gul's ears. "You'll like the new house," he promised. "There's no neighbor anywhere close, and there's a lake just in front of it. You're going to have fun."

It would probably be smarter to leave the boar here, but Frey couldn't do it. His sister might agree to take care of Gul, but she had other things to focus on, and besides, the boar was good company. Frey wasn't used to being on his own. Here in Asgard, there were gods everywhere, and they didn't think anything of visiting other gods. Frey had mostly kept to himself, visiting his sister and a few others but staying out of sight from Odin and his friends. It was never a good thing when Odin noticed you, so Frey had made sure that wouldn't happen.

At least until Loki had needed help.

Frey hadn't been able to stay away then. Loki was one of the few powerful gods in their pantheon who was nice to everyone, including minor gods. Frey considered him a friend and hadn't hesitated to step in when Loki needed him. Even now, he'd rather spend time with Loki than in Asgard, and while he wasn't sure he'd be able to, since Loki had just had a child, the sooner Frey got out of Asgard, the better it would be. He'd never lived in the human world before, but it couldn't be hard.

Could it?

"Frey?" a voice called out.

For a second, Frey wondered if Odin had found him. It was

a woman's voice, though, and there was only one woman who visited him regularly. "In the bedroom," he answered his sister.

She appeared a few moments later. They looked alike, with their long blond hair and green eyes. She was just a few inches shorter than he was, but her presence in the room was much bigger.

"What are you doing?" she asked, stroking Gul's head.

"Packing. I got a house in the human world." Frey would never hide anything from his sister. She was the one person in the entire world he trusted completely, including with this. Besides, he wanted her to be able to find him if she needed anything. She'd stayed out of what had happened with Loki, so hopefully, Odin would leave her alone, but just in case, Frey wanted her to know where he was.

Her eyes widened. "Why?"

"Do you really have to ask?"

She smiled just as the edges of Frey's vision wavered. He knew what that meant, and he reached out. He didn't have to say anything for Freya to understand what was about to happen, for which he was grateful. She grabbed his hand and pulled him close, and she was there to hold him up when the world around him turned dark.

For a few seconds, that was all he could see. Everywhere he looked, everything he could see was completely dark. It was as if the world around him had ceased to exist, and it wasn't something he was used to. He licked his lips, telling himself this was just a vision and that he didn't need to panic. Whatever he was seeing, it wasn't real.

Not yet, anyway.

A sound made him tense. It was a slithering, something he wasn't used to hearing. It seemed to come from everywhere at once, so he slowed down his breathing. Once he did, it was easier to hear that whatever was making that noise was coming toward him from the left. So that was where he turned. He had no idea what to expect, but it couldn't be good. Thankfully, this was a vision, which meant that whatever was coming wouldn't see him. Visions were always important, so he'd have to get as many details as he could. No matter how important they were, they were never easy to understand.

Something finally appeared. For the first few moments, it was only a light-colored shape. The closer it came, the more details Frey could see. The shape was a light yellow, and as it continued coming toward him, he realized what he was looking at.

A giant snake.

Frey was slammed out of the vision as quickly as he'd been brought in. He stumbled, his senses assaulted by the light and the smells that surrounded him, but Freya was there. She stood in front of him and cupped his cheeks with both her hands, forcing him to look at her.

"Breathe," she ordered.

He nodded and obeyed. They'd been dealing with this since they were children, so she knew what to do and say. She gave him the time he needed to breathe in and out, and once he was calmer, she released him.

"What did you see?" she asked.

He shook his head. "A giant snake."

She frowned. "What does that mean?"

"I have no idea." But something told Frey it wouldn't be good.

He could see the future, and it was never an easy gift to deal with. There were no explanations, no one to tell him how it worked and what the visions meant. He only had his own brain to rely on and help make sense of everything, but for now, there was nothing else he could get from the vision. The only thing he'd seen was a giant snake, and it could mean pretty much anything.

"You should leave as soon as possible," Freya murmured.

"I agree. I just need to grab some clothes and a few other things. I'll close the palace once I'm done, but it would be great if you could keep an eye on it."

"Of course. You'll tell me where you're going?"

"I already wrote down everything you need to know to find me on this," Frey said as he took out a piece of paper from his pocket.

Freya took it and looked down at it. "Finland?"

"Why not? I want to be alone, and I found the perfect house there."

"Does that mean I have to stay away?"

Frey was already shaking his head. "Never you. You're not the reason I'm leaving."

Odin, Thor, and their acolytes were, but something told Frey he'd have to face them somewhere down the line. The giant snake might have something to do with them, or it might not. Only the future would tell, and it wouldn't come any faster if Frey continued obsessing over it and the vision. So instead of doing that, he turned his mind back to packing.

He'd have time later to wonder what the giant snake had been all about.

CHAPTER TWO

R a still wasn't sure that going to the human world was the best idea. Ra still hadn't made a decision, but Nu had presented him with a gift a few days ago, and he hadn't been able to say no. When he'd opened it, it had taken him a moment to realize what he was holding.

He was holding it now, too, trying to make sense of it. He glided his finger along the screen, trying to find more news about the natural disasters, but every time he thought he'd gotten it, the screen changed, and something different opened. He had no idea what he was doing, but he wouldn't admit it to anyone. Besides, he doubted Nu could use this phone any better than he could.

No, if Ra wanted help, he'd have to get it somewhere else. What better place than the palace where Sed and Qebui lived?

They'd be surprised to see him, but that wouldn't be enough to stop Ra. The only thing that could was himself. He didn't know what he'd do in the human world, but even after rejecting Nu's idea of going there, he couldn't stop thinking about it.

What was there to hold him back? He'd spent the past millennia hiding away in his wing at the sky palace. He'd put more and more distance between himself and the other gods, and after a while, they'd left him alone. He enjoyed being on his own, but he hadn't realized back then that there could be such a thing as being on his own for too long. The loneliness had dug its claws into him, and it was hurting him and making him feel restless.

Besides, Ra refused to be scared of anything. He was one of the most powerful gods in his pantheon, possibly of all pantheons. He could face whatever was thrown at him, from other gods to humans. There was no reason for him not to visit the human world beyond the fact that he might not be interested, but he was. At the very least, it would be a change of scenery and would hopefully take away some of the boredom he'd been feeling. Maybe he could even investigate the natural disasters.

The thought of what might be happening to cause them made him nervous. He was more powerful than most gods, but that didn't mean nothing scared him. He could think of at least a few beings he never wanted to meet again, and he hoped none of them was behind the disasters.

Staring at the phone wouldn't help him understand how it worked, so Ra made his decision. He looked around his bedroom one last time, made sure he was dressed appropriately, and teleported to the palace where his two grandsons lived.

He had no idea where he was going. Since he'd never visited, he focused on them, hoping it would be enough. He arrived in a large room that seemed to be an office. The wide doors were opened, and a warm breeze touched his skin. There was no one behind the desk, but when he turned, he found two men on the couch. One of them was on top of the other, and they were kissing in a way that made Ra's stomach churn.

Once, he'd been capable of such passion. It had been a long time since he'd done what the two men were doing right now, though. He'd lost interest in it and in many other things.

He cleared his throat. He'd just ask where he could find his grandsons, then he'd get out of the office, and these two could go back to what they were doing.

The man on top squeaked and jumped away from the man on the couch. He tripped on the coffee table and started to tilt backward, but the other man grabbed him and helped him stay on his feet. Then they both turned to look at Ra, and he realized he wouldn't have to look for his grandsons.

He smiled at Qebui. "I apologize for interrupting you."

Qebui snorted. "It's fine."

Qebui's partner, Jimmy, was staring at Ra with wide eyes. They'd been introduced before, but they hadn't talked much. The human seemed wary of him and stunned, and Ra wasn't sure how to deal with that. He wanted to be treated normally, not like one of the fathers of his pantheon. If that was what he'd wanted, he'd have stayed in the sky palace.

And why was he calling the palace that now?

"What can we do for you?" Qebui asked as he straightened his white gown.

He kept his distance, and it took Ra a moment to realize that even Qebui was uncomfortable with his presence. He was sorry that his own family didn't want to spend time with him, but he didn't blame Qebui. Ra hadn't thought about the consequences when he'd retired and decided to stay away from the other gods. He should have, but back then, he'd felt that doing so was the only way for him to remain sane. Still, he didn't want his own family to keep him at arm's length. It would take work to show Qebui he didn't mean any harm, but hopefully, his presence would help.

"I wanted to talk to you," Ra explained.

"About what?"

Jimmy moved toward the door. "I'll ask someone to bring refreshments."

Ra started to tell him he didn't need to do that, but Qebui shook his head. He finally moved closer, and Ra understood why when he murmured, "Let him do that for you. It'll help him not be as intimidated."

Ra nodded. "Of course."

Things were still awkward as they sat around the coffee

table on which Jimmy had stumbled earlier. Ra stayed away from the couch, and he suspected Jimmy knew why, because his cheeks were red.

"We didn't expect you to come down to the human world," Qebui said once they were drinking mint tea.

"I didn't expect to come, but Nu suggested it."

That caused Jimmy to lean forward. "How are they?"

"Meddling, like always. They suggested I spend some time in the human world, but I don't know where to start. I tried using the phone they gave me to choose a place, but I'm useless with human technology." It cost Ra to admit that, but he was with family. Maybe making himself vulnerable would help Qebui and Jimmy relax.

"You can go wherever you want. Just choose a part of the world and explore it."

"I don't know where to start," Ra admitted.

To his surprise, Jimmy got to his feet and walked around the table. He sat on the arm of the armchair Ra was sitting in and wiggled his fingers. Ra was happy to hand over the phone, and he watched in awe as Jimmy quickly made sense of what was on the screen.

"There you go," Jimmy said. "This is the maps app. Why don't you close your eyes, point at the phone, and choose something?"

"I'd like a place that's nothing like Egypt."

Jimmy nodded. "Makes sense. You want to explore a place you don't know. Well, many places are different, but maybe somewhere cold? You could go to Canada or maybe Scandinavia." He touched the screen again, then held it out to Ra again. "There. Just point at a spot."

Ra wasn't sure this was the best way to do this, but he obeyed. Jimmy leaned closer, an excited expression on his face. It made Ra feel good to know that the human wasn't afraid of him anymore.

"Finland," Jimmy declared.

Ra blinked. "What's that?"

"It's in Europe. Pretty cold most of the year, and I'm sure that once you're over spending time with people, you'll find some pretty isolated places to spend time. How does that sound?"

Ra found himself beaming at the human. "It sounds perfect."

Finland was everything Frey could have wanted and had hoped for.

He loved the house he'd found, with its red wooden walls and tall grass. The inside was a bit sparse, but he had everything he needed and enjoyed living differently. Besides, if he needed something, he could use his powers to get it.

But he was enjoying his life as a human. He suspected most of the people he interacted with knew he was something more, but no one had said anything. Frey hadn't expected it, but he was relieved, and he'd decided to thank the people of the village where he lived. He didn't have much power, being a minor god, but he could help them with good harvests, healthy animals, and sunshine. Apparently, Finland didn't have much of that, and while Frey would have to be careful not to change the weather too much, he was enjoying himself. Finally, his powers came in handy. He could help people, something he hadn't believed he could do. He wasn't powerful enough and didn't have the right kind of influence.

But maybe he did.

A wet nose against his hand startled him. He looked down at Gul, who was trying to tell him something. Probably that he wanted to go for a swim in the lake.

Frey gestured at the wide expanse of water. "You know the way," he told the boar.

Gul grunted but stayed where he was. He was protective of Frey, something that had come in handy many times. Frey was grateful for the company and enjoyed playing and spending time with Gul.

"I promise I'll play with you later," Frey told the boar as he got to his feet.

He'd placed two chairs on the porch of his house, facing the lake. One had always been empty, and it would probably stay that way. That was perfectly fine with Frey, though. He'd left Asgard to stay away from the other gods. He doubted he could find companionship with a human, although weirder things had happened. He'd wait and see, and maybe, he'd make a few friends. Even if he didn't, he wouldn't be alone. He had Gul, but also Loki and his friends.

Gul stared up at him. Frey stroked his head.

"I have to go to the grocery store, but I'll be back soon. Maybe I'll even bring you some of that fish you like."

Gul seemed to understand that, and he perked up. When Frey stepped off the porch, the boar stayed where he was. He wasn't a pet, and he was smarter than a dog or cat. He knew he could go in anytime he wanted, but also that he was allowed to roam. They didn't have close neighbors, so he had plenty of space to enjoy himself, and he could always get into the house if that was what he wished for. Frey gave him all the freedom he wanted, and it had worked well so far. Gul had never felt the need to leave him, and Frey hoped he never would.

The village wasn't distant, and although it was cold, Frey enjoyed walking. He made his way toward the grocery store, mentally thinking about what he had to buy. The fish for Gul, of course, but he'd found out he rather liked hot chocolate, so he'd get that, too. He could have gotten everything without going to the grocery store, but Frey enjoyed living like a human. It gave him something to do and made him feel like he wasn't quite as alone as he'd always thought. It didn't matter that the humans of the village suspected he was a god. They'd never treated him any differently, and he liked that. He wanted more of it, which was why he went to the grocery store every few days.

He walked past his nearest neighbor's house and noticed she was tending to her plants. He still didn't understand how they could survive the cold, but maybe he could try planting some once he was used to living in his house. He waved, and the neighbor waved back. They'd never talked, but they knew who each other was, and that was enough for Frey to feel a kind of kinship with her.

The village was close, and Frey had warmed up by the time he got there. He'd also crossed paths with several humans, and he'd smiled and nodded at all of them. He could talk to them, but they seemed to prefer if he kept his distance, and that was perfectly fine with him. He was here to be alone, and while it was nice to have company sometimes, now wasn't one of those times.

The grocery store was a delight. Frey knew there were bigger ones in bigger towns, but he was perfectly happy with what he could find here. Shopping here made him feel normal, and that was one more thing he enjoyed.

He hadn't been entirely sure that moving to the human world was a good idea, but he was glad he had. Eventually, Odin would realize he wasn't around anymore and would come to find him, but for now, Frey could live his life the way he wanted. He didn't have to bow down to Odin and do what he asked. Odin would easily beat Frey in a fight, but hopefully, he wouldn't have a reason to remember that Frey even existed. Whatever he was plotting, it couldn't be a good thing, but it didn't involve Frey.

And that was why Frey had left Asgard. He wanted nothing to do with the gods there, especially the ones in charge.

He'd be perfectly fine never going back.

No matter how unlikely that was, he could always hope, right?

Ra hadn't known what to expect from Finland, but when he got there, he got a shock. He knew what snow was, but he hadn't thought he'd see a smattering of it on the ground. Everywhere he looked was white instead of the yellow of the sand he was used to. It was also much colder than he was used to, but thankfully, Jimmy had expected that, and he'd made sure Ra wore a jacket. Even with it on, Ra could feel the cold sinking into his bones.

He loved it.

He wasn't sure where he was. He could see a lake close by, and right in front of him, a long white building. There were a couple houses behind him, both of them painted red. The thing he enjoyed the most were the trees, though. He knew palm trees, of course, but these weren't palm trees. Their leaves were green in some cases, yellow and brown in others, and they were beautiful.

Since he had no idea where he was, he decided to walk. It would be the best way for him to find his way around and maybe a place to stay. He hadn't thought much about what he'd do once he was here, but he was ready to find out if Finland could be a home for him the same way the sky palace had been.

He walked down the street, his gaze still on the trees surrounding him. He passed more houses and several people walking down the road or in their yards. All of them gave him a wide berth, but he wasn't surprised. He looked different, and not just physically. He was dressed differently, too, and it soon became obvious to him he should have known better. He had a jacket on, but it was nowhere near warm enough for the weather. His shoes weren't made for snow, and he suspected he wouldn't be able to save them once his walk was over.

But he was delighted. He was walking along the lake, and the water glittered in the weak sunlight on his left. The lake appeared endless, even though Ra doubted that was the case. He could see himself living here, though.

He came to a crossroads and decided to go straight ahead. He hadn't seen many cars yet, and he wondered how many people lived here. Not a lot, which was what he was looking for. He wanted a change, but that didn't mean he was willing to live in a crowd of humans.

He continued walking until he reached a more inhabited area. It was close to the lake still, and he already knew he wanted to find a place to stay by the water. He didn't know where to find a home, but he'd have to start talking to people, so he turned right, heading for what might be the center of this town. The buildings here were taller, and he didn't want to live in one of these places, but finding humans would help him find what he was looking for.

There were more people now, and Ra was delighted at the way the children looked at him. They didn't have the same fear as their parents, and they waved to get his attention. Ra had always loved children. When they were young, they were uncomplicated. It was when they started growing up that things became harder.

Ra waved at the children, ignoring the way their parents pulled them away. He knew humans could tell he was more than them, that he had power crackling under his skin. They were smart, no matter what some of the gods believed.

But wandering in town didn't help him. When he tried talking to people, they steered away. He wouldn't get help from them, which meant he was on his own, or rather, that he'd have to call Jimmy. The human had told him to call if he needed anything, and while Ra had wanted to brush him off, he was glad he hadn't. He might be a powerful god, but he had no idea how to deal with the human world. To help him with that, he'd need a human.

So instead of scaring the humans in town, Ra turned around and headed back toward the lake. He continued walking on the road that appeared to circle it, eager to explore and see everything he could find. He already loved this place, and he'd only been here a couple of hours. It was easy to imagine himself living here for the long term. It couldn't be more different from Egypt or the sky palace, and that was what he loved about it.

He didn't know how long he walked, but the houses became fewer and fewer as he did so. He found himself closer to the lake, surrounded by trees, nature, and little else. There was a white house in front of him, but he hadn't passed any cars, and he wondered if he would. He'd be fine with not meeting humans, but eventually, he'd have to find a place to settle down.

That was when he noticed someone walking toward him. The figure wasn't tall, but the sun glittered on their blond hair. They were carrying two bags, and as they moved closer to each other, Ra realized they'd been to the store.

And whoever this was, was a god.

Ra stopped moving, staring at the man coming toward him. Ra hadn't recognized him from a distance, but now that they were closer, he thought he'd met him. It didn't take him long to remember where. It had been recently, after all, and the other god had made an impression on Ra. Ra had believed he was done with physical attraction, but he'd been drawn toward this man.

He still was.

How could he not be? The man was shorter than Ra, but Ra thought they'd fit together perfectly. He wanted nothing more than to run his fingers through the man's long blond hair, to see passion in what he remembered were green eyes. He wanted the man's thin, strong body under his. He wanted to hear every single sound they could make together.

But the man had noticed him, and he moved more cautiously now. Ra decided to wait where he was and see what would happen. He didn't have to wait long, anyway. After a few minutes, the other god came to a stop in front of Ra and put down his grocery bags.

"Ra," the god said.

"We met recently, but I don't remember your name. I apologize."

Thankfully, the other god didn't seem offended. He smiled and tilted his head forward. "Of course. It wasn't the best situation to make friends. I'm Frey."

Ra slightly bowed, too. He could feel the power coming from Frey, so he knew he was the most powerful of them. That didn't mean he wanted to anger a god from another pantheon.

Until recently, he'd never dealt with any of them. He had more than enough trouble with his own pantheon, and he'd retired anyway. It had been a shock when Nu had decided to help their friend Loki, and Frey had been there, so Ra knew he was part of Loki's family.

"I don't mean to be rude, but what are you doing here?" Frey asked.

Ra found himself smiling. "I wanted a change of scenery."

Frey's eyebrows shut up. "And you thought Finland would be the best place to visit? There's snow on the ground."

"I have to admit I didn't expect it, but I should have."

"Of course you should have. This is *Finland*." Frey looked around. "Are you here on your own?"

"I am, and I'm looking for a place to stay." Surely, Frey would help a fellow god? Especially since they'd fought together to save Loki from the cave he'd been imprisoned in.

"Let me guess. You arrived with no plan and no knowledge of this place."

"I did. I realize I should, at the very least, have planned where I'd be staying, but if it comes to that, I can always go back to the palace."

"But you're here for a reason."

"As are you."

Ra could only begin to imagine why Frey was here. He suspected it was something similar to his own reason, though. Over the millennia, many gods decided to strike out on their own. Many of them preferred staying in their palace, away from humans, but just as many needed to be away from other gods. There was no better place for that than the human world, and Ra wouldn't be surprised to discover that many gods lived here. Frey seemed to be one of them, and while Ra hadn't expected to meet a god in this remote area of the world, he couldn't say he was sorry. He needed help, and he wouldn't say no if Frey offered it to him.

He wasn't here to make friends, but if Frey was nice enough to offer friendship to him, Ra wouldn't say no.

Frey shouldn't have been amused, but he was. He'd only barely met Ra when they'd rescued Loki, then later, when they'd met after Loki had given birth. He didn't think they'd ever talked, and he'd done his best to stay away from the other god, even though he was more than a little attracted to him.

He hadn't stayed away because they belonged to a different pantheon. He'd stayed away because Ra was much more powerful than him, and he hadn't wanted to risk anything happening. Now, though, Ra didn't look like a powerful god. His powers were still there, crackling in the air, but he was lost, and Frey was the only one who could help him.

He wasn't about to say no.

Ra was incredibly attractive, and Frey would have tried to convince him to climb into his bed in any other circumstance. Ra's hair was the darkest Frey had ever seen, a black that glinted almost blue in the sunlight. His eyes were just as dark as they stared at Frey, sending a shiver down his spine. Ra's full attention was on Frey, something he wasn't used to, especially coming from such a powerful god. He didn't understand why Ra was so interested in him, although maybe that was because he needed help.

Frey wasn't surprised. Finland wasn't Ra's usual abode. He didn't understand why Ra was here, but he wouldn't be the one telling him to leave.

He *would* be the one telling him to buy more clothes, though.

He cleared his throat. "If you're going to stick around, you'll need different clothes."

Ra looked down at himself. "You don't like what I'm wearing?"

Frey made a strangled sound. If anything, he liked it too much. Ra wore white suit pants, along with a white vest. The shirt under the vest was black, as was the open jacket that hung on his shoulders. He hadn't put his arms through it like anyone else would have. The jacket was just there, looking as if it might slide off at any second.

If all of that hadn't been hot enough, the fact that Ra had rolled up his sleeves to expose his forearms made Frey feel weak in the knees. Ra wore golden bracelets on both wrists, and a golden necklace hung from his neck. Frey recognized an Egyptian symbol, just like the one on Ra's black belt.

And Frey really shouldn't be looking at Ra's belt or anywhere in that area.

"You're going to freeze if you don't find warmer clothing,"

he explained.

"I'm a god. We don't freeze."

That was true enough. Frey clearly shouldn't be worried, but he still was. It didn't matter that Ra was like a fish out of water. Whatever happened, he could get himself out of trouble.

Frey had no idea what to think about this. He couldn't help but wonder if Ra had hidden reasons to be here, maybe related to Frey's visions. The snake Frey kept seeing wasn't a normal animal. It was enormous, and Frey wouldn't be having visions of a normal animal. The snake had to be a god, or at the very least, related to a pantheon, and there were no snakes in Frey's. He suspected there were plenty of snakes in Ra's, but how would Ra know about the visions? The only person Frey had explained the visions to was his sister, and she'd never have told anyone.

He wasn't about to bring up the visions. It didn't matter if Ra was here for those or not. They weren't friends, and Frey doubted they ever would be.

He grabbed his grocery bags, ready to go home. "You need to turn around and go back to town. You'll find stores there to buy warmer clothing, or maybe you should go back to your palace and plan this better."

Ra frowned. "You're leaving?"

"I have to get back home. It was good to see you." And it had been, even though none of this made sense.

Whatever reason Ra had to be here, he'd helped Loki when Loki needed him, and that meant Frey considered him a friend, or at the very least, someone on his side. Gods changed their minds easily and quickly, though, so it might have changed by the next time they met. They could be enemies then, even though they weren't now.

Ra nodded. "It was nice talking to you. I didn't expect to meet another god here, but I'm glad I did. It helps me feel not quite as out of place."

There was nothing Ra could do *not* to be out of place here, but Frey didn't say that out loud. Instead, he nodded and started walking again.

He could feel Ra's gaze on his back, but he forced himself to stare ahead. It didn't matter how attracted he was to the other god. His life was already complicated enough, and he'd come here to uncomplicate it. No matter how gorgeous he was, falling into bed with Ra wouldn't help Frey find what he was looking for.

But still, he wondered if maybe Loki knew something. It wouldn't hurt to ask, right? Frey could stay vague, mention he'd recently seen Ra, and see what Loki had to say about it.

Or he could just visit Loki and not mention Ra at all. It had been several weeks since he'd seen Loki and his family, and he missed them more than he'd expected. What happened to Loki in the months after that had pulled him and Frey closer, and they'd become better friends. Frey was here to be by himself and away from other gods, but not from *all* other gods. Loki was one of the few he was planning on having a relationship with, and Loki was always happy to see him.

Hopefully, he'd be happy today, too. Maybe Frey could offer himself as a babysitter once he had the answers he was looking for.

CHAPTER THREE

Frey was sitting on his porch when he noticed his nearest neighbor walking by the lake. He stared at her for a moment, surprised to see her. He'd been alone since his trip to see Loki a few days ago, and he'd almost forgotten he lived amongst humans. Luckily, Gul was inside the house sleeping, so he wouldn't scare her. Gul would never attack someone unless Frey needed help, but Frey didn't expect humans to understand that.

When she looked up and their gazes crossed, he waved at her. He expected things to stop there, but instead, to his surprise, she made a beeline toward him. He stared at her, wondering what had happened. They'd never talked to each other. They knew each other from afar and waved when they crossed paths, but that was it. Frey wanted things to remain that way, but maybe, she didn't.

He got to his feet and waited for her to reach him. She seemed in a hurry, and Frey wondered if someone was in danger. It didn't make sense, though. Why would anyone in this small town be in danger? Maybe she wanted something. Frey had no doubt she was aware of the fact that he was a god, as was everyone he'd met since he'd moved here. It wouldn't be unheard of for some people to come to him because they needed something, and while Frey was happy to listen to them, he wouldn't make promises.

His neighbor finally reached him, and he smiled in welcome. She wore a heavy red jacket, and a hat covered her white hair. Her boots were sturdy, and the soles were covered in snow. She made Frey think of Ra and how unprepared he'd been for this weather.

There still wasn't much snow on the ground, but Frey suspected it wouldn't last long. From what he'd been told at the grocery store, usually by this time of year, the snow was thick and falling daily. He didn't like that things were different this year, and he wondered if he could ask someone for godly help. His power worked on the sun, but not on the snow.

His neighbor placed her hands on her hips and stared at him. "Are you friends with that strange man?" she asked in heavily accented English.

Frey blinked. "What strange man?"

"The one with black hair. He's been seen around town."

She could only be talking about Ra. Had he gotten himself in trouble? Frey doubted he'd been hurt. He was a god—a powerful one. It would be strange if humans went anywhere near him, although Frey supposed that some humans were drawn by gods rather than scared.

"I know him," he said cautiously.

"What does he want from us?"

"I don't know. Maybe the same thing I want."

She squinted. "But you've been staying here alone. He hasn't."

"You said he's in town?"

She nodded curtly. "He's talking to people. They're afraid of him."

"I don't think he's here to hurt anyone."

"It doesn't matter. He is what he is, and we're scared."

Frey felt sorry for Ra. He was here because he wanted to change his life, but it would be near impossible for humans to accept him. It was easier for Frey because he was much less powerful, but there was no way to ignore Ra.

Ra was a sun god. He was revered as such, but not here. The people in this country had their own gods, which probably made things even harder for them. If Ra was going to stick around, he'd need to find an isolated place and stick to it like Frey was. It might not be fair, but it was what it was, and they both needed to accept it. Frey had always known he wouldn't be able to live amongst humans. Was Ra aware of that? Or was he here because he wanted to attempt just that? It wouldn't work with how powerful he was, and maybe he needed someone to tell him.

Frey had hoped Loki would have answers for him, but he hadn't. He'd been happy to see Frey and even more so to let Frey babysit while he took Sam out for dinner, but he and Ra weren't friends. He hadn't even known Ra had left the sky palace, which meant that if Frey wanted answers to his questions, he'd have to go straight to the source.

To Ra.

"Can you talk to him?" Frey's neighbor asked. "We just want to be left alone."

"I'll see what I can do."

She stared at him for a moment before nodding. "Thank you."

"I'm not making promises. He's much more powerful than I am."

"That's why we're uncomfortable with him."

Frey's neighbor slightly bowed her head before turning around. Frey watched her go, wondering what he was supposed to do now. He might not have made promises, but he'd said he'd talk to Ra, which meant he'd have to do just that. First, though, he wanted to know what Loki thought of it.

He took his phone out of his pocket and unlocked the screen. Loki and Freya were the only people Frey called regularly, but he enjoyed technology. The phone helped him be less bored than he would have been otherwise.

As he waited for Loki to answer, he got ready to go to town. He already had his boots on, so he only needed his jacket and to check on Gul. The boar was sleeping by the fire, so Frey left him to it.

"Frey!" Loki exclaimed. "Sorry it took me so long to answer."

"Don't worry about it. I'm sure you're busy."

"I didn't remember children needed so much attention."

Frey found himself smiling. "But you love it." Even though the baby had been unexpected, both Loki and Sam were absolutely in love with him. It was good to see, and it made Frey wonder if he might want another child. It had been a long time since he'd been a father, and he didn't have anyone to have a child with, but maybe he didn't need anyone.

"I do," Loki said.

Frey could almost see the smile on his face. "It's good to hear you so happy."

"I *am* happy, and I want you to be, too. What's going on?"

"I had a visitor. Apparently, Ra is freaking out everyone in town, and they want me to do something about it."

Loki chuckled. "Of course they do. Don't they know how much more powerful he is than you?"

There was no hint of nastiness in Loki's voice. The fact that Ra was more powerful was just that—a fact. It didn't say anything about Frey or Ra themselves, but some gods looked down on less powerful gods. Loki had never been that kind of god.

"I'm sure they're aware of it, but I'm still the best person to do something around here."

"And how can I help you?"

"Do you have any tips? I know you're not close to Ra, but you know him better than I do."

Loki chuckled. "Frankly, I don't. I would never have expected him to do something like this. I think you should treat him like you would anyone else, though."

"But he's not anyone else. He could kill me with barely a

thought."

"I might not know him well, but he won't do that. Why is he in Finland, though? Isn't it so he can live amongst humans and stay away from other gods?"

"Possibly."

"Then treat him like a human."

"It's not like I have human friends."

"You have Sam. But fine. Talk to Ra as if you were talking to me. I'm much more powerful than you, but you've never had a problem telling me what's on your mind."

"That's because you're family."

"In a way, so is Ra. It's acquired family, but family, none-theless. I don't think Ra is there to hurt anyone. I'll call Nu and ask them about him if it makes you feel better."

"It would." It wouldn't help Frey, but at least he'd know more about Ra and his reason for being here.

He hadn't been able to stop thinking about the other god since they'd met on the road. Frey had many questions but hadn't allowed himself to ask even one of them. Maybe this time, he could, and he'd discover why Ra was here.

Ra peered around, not knowing where to start. He didn't need to eat, and if he really wanted to, he could go back to the sky palace, or even to the palace where Qebui and Sed lived. He had no doubt someone there would feed him, but that wasn't what he wanted. He was here to be alone, and he needed to manage things on his own.

Of course, that would be much easier if he had a place to stay.

He'd spent the past few days roaming around town. He'd bought new clothing, but most humans seemed terrified of him, and he hadn't managed to find a home yet. When the night came, he continued walking the streets. He enjoyed it, and he didn't need rest, anyway. He'd been all over town, though, and he knew he wanted to stay. But he had no idea how to make things work with humans.

Maybe standing in the middle of the tiny grocery store wasn't the best idea.

Ra had never been in a grocery store. He hadn't even been sure what they were used for until he walked in, but then he'd realized this was where humans bought their food. He didn't recognize anything on the shelves, and that made him want to grab one of every item and taste them. He doubted the humans would take nicely to that, though, so he'd grabbed a basket and chose only the things he *really* wanted to try. Still, everyone in the store was staring.

Ra was used to it, but he'd hoped things would be different here. He supposed he should have known better. Humans knew the gods, but not many of them ever encountered them, especially not someone as powerful as Ra. It was normal that they didn't know how to behave or what to say, and Ra didn't hold it against them. He just wished they'd stop staring.

It was starting to make him uncomfortable, so he carried his basket toward the front of the store. He watched as humans put their purchases on the counter, so he did the same, not knowing what to expect. The woman sitting behind the counter stared at him with wide eyes, but she picked up everything Ra wanted to purchase and pushed it forward after making it to do a beeping sound. Ra grabbed one of the bags under the counter like he'd seen others do and started putting his things into it, but once the woman had pushed everything his way, she said something he didn't understand. He cocked his head at her, and she leaned back as if she feared he'd hurt her.

"She wants money," a voice said behind Ra.

He turned to find Frey standing there. "Money?"

For some reason, Frey seemed amused. "You're in a

grocery store."

"It's where humans get their food."

"It is, but they don't get it for free. She's asking you for payment."

Ra was lost. "I don't have money."

Thankfully, Frey didn't seem annoyed. Instead, he pushed past Ra and toward the lady. "I'll take care of it."

He listened as Frey and the woman talked in her language, and he tried to understand, but he couldn't. If he was going to stick around, he'd need to learn quickly. He didn't want to be clueless.

Frey grabbed one of the bags and headed toward the exit, so Ra took the other and quickly followed him. "Thank you," he said once they were both outside.

Frey smiled at him. "You're welcome. Considering how unprepared you were, I should have expected something like this to happen."

"I should have done more research. I'm sorry you had to come to my aid."

"It's fine. I'd like to know what you're doing here, though."

"I already told you."

"You told me you wanted to live here but not why." Frey hesitated. "You don't have to if you'd rather not, but the humans around here are worried. My neighbor came to me and asked me to do something about you."

Ra frowned. "I didn't mean to scare anyone."

"I know. Let's be honest, though. It was bound to happen because of who you are and how powerful you are."

Ra didn't like the sound of that. "I just wanted a change."

"From the sky palace?"

Why did Frey call it that, too? "Yes. I've lived there for millennia, and it's become too much."

Frey nodded. "I'm not surprised."

"It's why you're here, too?"

"In part. I do understand why you decided you needed a change, but is staying here the best idea?"

"Any other place would be the same. If I'd stayed in Egypt, people would treat me differently, while I want a normal life like all humans."

"The people here *are* treating you differently. They might not know who you are precisely, but they can feel how powerful you are."

Ra had been afraid of that. He wanted to be treated like anyone else. Was that too much to ask?

He knew how lucky he was. He hadn't just been born a god. He'd been born the most powerful god in his pantheon, which came with advantages he wouldn't have had otherwise. It also came with a heavy responsibility, though, and when he'd retired, he'd wanted to stay away from that. He still did.

Frey sighed. "Look, I understand why you feel this way, but if you want to stay, you'll have to make changes. For one, you shouldn't be roaming on your own. You don't know much about the human world, and it shows."

"I agree, but who could I talk to?"

"How about another god?"

"No one in my pantheon will talk to me." That wasn't exactly true, but Ra would rather not ask Qebui and Sed about this, even though they were used to living with humans.

"How about Loki? I called him before coming to find you, and I'm sure he'll be happy to talk to you."

"We don't know each other."

"But you're Nu's son, and besides, you were there to help Loki when he was in that cave. He remembers that. I'm sure you could become friends if you give it time."

Ra had never been close to anyone outside his pantheon, but now that he thought of it, he'd never been close to anyone *in* his pantheon, either. He wanted to change, and nothing stopped him from becoming friends with Loki or Frey. He was aware that he needed help, and who better than them to do that? They seemed to be used to the human world, while he wasn't.

"I'll talk to Loki," he said.

Frey smiled. "Great. Let's head there now."

Ra blinked. "I'm sure he has better things to do than to talk to me."

"Trust me. He doesn't. He'll welcome the distraction. He's not used to spending all his time alone with the baby, and Sam had to return to work."

Ra cocked his head. "Why does he work? Loki could give him anything he wants without him having to work."

"Some humans like to work, while others want to feel useful."

There was a big difference between gods and humans, and while Ra had been aware of that before, spending time in the human world made it even more obvious. He needed help, and he needed it as soon as possible. "Let's visit Loki, then."

Frey wouldn't say he didn't like Ra, but he had no idea how to deal with him. That was one of the reasons he was glad when they got to Loki's home. Loki would fix Ra, and Frey could go home and not worry about him again.

He should have known things wouldn't go that way.

As soon as he stepped into the house, Loki dumped his crying son into Frey's arms. Frey looked down at the baby, wondering what was happening and what he was supposed to do with him.

"There's your uncle Frey," Loki was saying. "You've missed him, haven't you?"

"I think he's too young to miss anyone, let alone someone he's seen only a few times," Frey pointed out. He lifted Hodr, trying to place him back into Loki's arms.

Instead of taking his son, Loki took a step back.

Frey glared at him. "What are you doing? This is your son, not mine. You're the one who should take care of him."

"I *have* been taking care of him. But he keeps crying, and I have no idea how to deal with it. I'm reaching the end of my patience."

"It doesn't mean you can dump him on me. What am I supposed to do with him? I don't know how to deal with children."

"I seem to remember you were quite good with your son."

"That was hundreds of years ago."

"But I'm sure you still know how to deal with children. Besides, look. He's not crying anymore."

That much was true, although Frey didn't know if it was because of him or because of something else. He doubted he could have this kind of influence on the baby.

But Loki had already moved on. His attention was on Ra, who hovered behind Frey, looking uncomfortable. That was probably how he felt, too. *Frey* was uncomfortable, and he knew Loki better than most people.

"I have to say, I didn't expect to see you here," Loki told Ra.

"That makes two of us," Ra drawled. "It's good to see you're doing well, though."

Loki beamed. "And it's thanks to you, at least in part. You helped me, and I'm eager to help you. Why don't you tell me what's going on?"

Loki guided Ra toward the living room, and Frey followed. Thankfully, the baby looked like he was falling asleep, so Frey hoped he wouldn't have to babysit for much longer. He loved the little guy, but he felt awkward holding him.

Loki gestured at the couches. "Sit down and tell me everything," he told Ra as he lowered himself onto one of the couches.

Before Ra could say anything, Loki was already bouncing up again.

"Wait. I'll grab some drinks, maybe snacks, too. I don't know about you, but I'm starving."

He left the living room quickly, abandoning Frey with a clueless god and a sleeping child.

Frey sat on the couch, careful not to wake the baby. He could feel Ra watching him, but he didn't look up until he was sure he was settled.

"What?" he asked when he did so.

"You look good with a baby in your arms."

Frey spluttered. "What does that mean?"

"Nothing that I haven't said. You seem good with children."

Frey wasn't sure that was so, but he had no idea how to answer. What was Ra talking about? Frey wasn't good with children. He was pretty sure the baby had already been half on his way to sleep when Loki dumped him into his arms, so he hadn't done anything weird.

He leaned down and pressed a kiss on top of the baby's head. He inhaled Hodr's sweet scent, trying to come up with an answer, but was unable to do so. Thankfully he didn't have to worry because Loki came back into the room, carrying a tray. When he put it down on the coffee table, Frey rolled his eyes. Loki had filled the tray with four different kinds of chips and five cans of soda, but of course, he'd forgotten glasses.

Loki looked at the tray. "Sam and I have to go grocery shopping. I could use my magic to get whatever you want, though."

"This is perfectly fine, thank you," Ra said, slightly bowing his head.

He looked regal, which Frey supposed made sense. Ra was one of the oldest Egyptian gods, possibly the second oldest after his parent, Nu. He'd been kind of a king to the other gods who'd been born since then, which would explain why he'd retired. Frey would have, too, with all those responsibilities and obligations on his shoulders.

Loki sat down again, and Frey waited to see if he'd get back to his feet. Thankfully, he didn't, instead grabbing one of the small bowls of chips to snack on as he listened to Ra.

"So, what's up?" he asked.

Frey resisted the urge to roll his eyes again. Loki had always behaved more like a human than a god, but it had worsened since he and Sam had gotten together. Frey suspected it had nothing to do with Sam and everything to do with the fact that Loki was spending more time in the human world.

Or maybe that wasn't true. Loki had been spending more than enough time in the human world before, too. He was more relaxed now, almost as if he finally felt he belonged. Frey yearned to feel that way, but so far, he hadn't been able to find a place for himself. His small house in Finland was close, and maybe he did belong there, but *who* did he belong with?

"I'm not sure why everyone thinks there's a problem," Ra said. "I've decided to move to the human world permanently. I think I'm doing pretty well, considering everything."

Loki turned his attention to Frey. "Is he?"

Frey shrugged one shoulder. "I've seen worse, but I've also seen much better."

"I don't have any kind of experience with humans," Ra said. "I've been doing my best to learn and thought I was doing well."

"Where are you living?" Frey asked him.

Ra looked away. Frey bit his lower lip so he wouldn't smile like an idiot. He'd known Ra was lying.

"I haven't found a home yet, but I'm looking for one."

Frey glanced at Loki. He hoped Loki would convince Ra to

go home, since he clearly wasn't in his element in the human world. It would make sense for him to head back to what everyone called the sky palace.

But of course, that wasn't how things went. Loki loved to disappoint people and do the opposite of what they wanted from him.

He grinned like an idiot. "Where do you want to live?"

"I quite like Finland," Ra told him, leaning forward. "It's so very different from Egypt, and I needed that."

"Oh, it's beautiful. I understand why you chose it, although the cold isn't for me. I think you'll do just fine there, though."

Frey made a strangled sound. "But maybe Ra would be more comfortable back in his palace with the other gods. Humans aren't taking well to him and his presence in town," he said slowly, staring at Loki and hoping he'd understand.

Loki waved Frey's words away. "Most humans will never understand us or how to deal with us. We can't think of them when we decide where to live. Sure, it's nice to have human friends and people who aren't afraid of you but depending on what you want from life, it's fine to be alone and stay away from everyone."

Ra nodded eagerly. "I'm done with the palace. I can't deal with my family one second longer."

Loki laughed. "I know how that feels. I hate most of my family, and they hate me right back. Frey is one of the exceptions, and I wouldn't give him up for anything. He makes a good babysitter."

Ra's gaze moved back to Frey. "I'm sure he does."

"But anyway, if you've decided to stay in the human world, you'll need to learn how to deal with them quickly. I could help you with that. I have my boyfriend and my son, of course, but I'm sure I can find time for you."

"I'd be eternally grateful."

Loki laughed again. "I don't need you to be. I like spending time with humans, and I quite like you, too."

That seemed to please Ra. Frey, on the other hand, wished Loki weren't so open about all of this. Frey had expected him to tell Ra to go home, but instead, he gave Ra more reasons to stay. The problem was that Loki would spend time with Ra, then go home. Frey was right there, though, and he'd have to deal with whatever mess the two of them left behind, including talking with the humans wary of Ra.

But he couldn't let Ra just roam around town as he'd been. He was freaking out the humans, and nothing good could come out of that for either of them.

He sighed. He'd have to be the adult in this situation.

Ra was delighted when Sam came home. He hadn't met many humans, but most of them were wary of him, if not outright scared. Even Sed and Qebui's partners kept their distance from Ra, but not Sam. No, Sam treated Ra as if he were just another friend, which was one of the reasons Ra had left the palace. He didn't want to be bowed down to and catered to.

They were still sitting on the couches in the living room, but now Sam was holding his son. Frey had appeared happy to give up the responsibility, but Ra suspected he'd enjoyed having the baby in his arms. Ra hadn't been lying when he'd said that Frey looked good with a child. Loki had mentioned something about Frey having children, and Ra wanted to ask, but it was better not to. Frey was a god, and more often than not, gods' lives were difficult and challenging. They lost many people, including children. If that was what had happened to Frey's child, Ra didn't want to be the one to reopen the wound. Besides, he still had his phone. He could do some research once he was alone.

Something landed in his lap, startling him. He looked

down at the cat, unsure what to do with it. The only other cat he had regular contact with was Nu's, and that cat wasn't anything like this one. For one, this cat had fur rather than bandages. Would it affect its behavior?

"That's Misty," Sam said.

"Is it all right if I pet her?"

Sam chuckled. "More than. She'll probably start yowling if you don't. She's a princess like that."

"And who am I not to give a princess what she wants," Ra murmured as he ran his fingertips down Misty's back.

The cat instantly started purring. She dug her claws into Ra's thighs, making him wince, but he was happy to have her there. He was even happier when she curled into his lap after kneading his thighs, and he continued stroking her.

When he looked up, everyone was staring at him.

He swallowed, wondering if he'd done something wrong. "I can put her down," he offered.

Loki shook his head. "There's no need for you to. Like Sam said, she's a princess, and the entire house is hers. Apparently, that includes your lap."

It was nice to be part of this group, even though Ra felt he missed many things as he listened to the conversations. He didn't know most of the people Loki and Frey were talking about, but Sam didn't seem to know them, either. He was focused on his son, and Ra decided to focus on the cat. He did exactly that until he heard what Frey was saying.

"I have no idea what the giant snake means. It's not unusual for me to have visions I can't explain, but I'm getting worried."

Loki hummed. "You think that snake has something to do with the natural disasters?"

"What are the odds it doesn't? Earthquakes and storms are happening left and right, and I keep having visions of a giant snake. They started at about the same time as that first earthquake, too. I can't believe it's just a coincidence."

"What are you going to do about it?"

"There's not much I *can* do. I've tried exploring the visions when I have them, but the only thing I can see is a giant snake. Everything else is completely dark, and it's not giving me any hints as to what's happening."

Ra turned the words in his mind. A giant snake and natural disasters like earthquakes and storms couldn't be a coincidence, but Ra was afraid of what it could mean if it wasn't. There was only one person he could think of that could have that kind of power, but he wasn't supposed to have it in the underworld. If Apophis was doing this, it meant he was becoming stronger and possibly trying to rise.

That would be a disaster for the entire human world and every single pantheon.

Ra swallowed and looked down at the cat. It couldn't be Apophis. He was stuck in the underworld, and there was no way out for him. What if he had help, though?

But Ra couldn't believe he did. What god would be stupid enough to help Apophis? Every god in the Egyptian pantheon knew what Apophis had done and that he'd do it again if he were free. Why would any of them help him?

Ra couldn't avoid thinking that what Frey was describing seemed like Apophis. He was known as a giant snake, after all. He was the god of chaos — even though he wasn't exactly a god.

"You need to stay away," he said out loud.

Frey blinked at him. "Away from what?"

"The snake."

"You mean from the vision? Do you know who that is?"

Ra shook his head. "I can't be sure."

"But you have an idea."

Ra hesitated. Apophis was his problem. He shouldn't involve gods from another pantheon in this mess, especially if

Apophis was at the center of it. Could he really push these gods away? They were his friends, and if Apophis was trying to return, Ra would need all the help he could find. His pantheon had supported him the first time he'd pushed Apophis back into the underworld. Things had degraded between the gods since then, and he wasn't sure he could get everyone on board again. He might need help from someone else, and for now, the only people he could think of were Loki and Frey and possibly the rest of their friends. There was no way to know if they'd be enough, but it was better than Ra facing Apophis on his own.

"I suspect it might be Apophis," he explained.

"You're going to have to give us more details," Loki said.

"He's one of the most ancient Egyptian deities," Ra told him. "He's not exactly part of our pantheon, but he's considered the god of chaos and always appeared as a giant serpent."

Frey was nodding. "And you think he's the serpent I'm seeing."

"I don't know who else it could be. Of course, the serpent you're seeing might belong to another pantheon."

"If that's the case, it's not from ours. We don't have snakes that I know of."

"What happened with Apophis?" Loki asked.

"He tried to take over the mortal world. He belongs in the underworld, but he's never been content with that. He kept trying, and eventually, I trapped him in the underworld. I had a lot of help, and I ensured he could never leave, but I'm starting to wonder."

"You think he's getting free."

"I don't know how that would be possible, but it might be the case, yes."

"What will happen if he does?"

Ra swallowed. "Nothing good."

The room was silent for so long that Ra wondered what everyone was thinking. Their expressions were grim, and they mirrored his own. Even if this was only a suspicion, it wasn't a good one. If Apophis was trying to escape the underworld, everyone was in trouble.

Frey sighed heavily. "What do we do, then?"

"The two of you should stay together," Loki said.

Frey didn't look happy. "Why?"

"Because you keep having visions of a giant snake, and Ra thinks he knows who that snake is. If he stays with you, you'll be able to go to him anytime you have the vision. He might be able to help identify the snake and whatever's happening. If this snake *is* Apophis and the situation is as disastrous as Ra believes, we need to know what's going on as soon as possible."

Ra doubted it would help, but he could do nothing but nod. If Apophis was trying to get out of the underworld, they'd have to face him eventually. To do so, they'd need to stand together, shoulder to shoulder, to protect the human world and the world as everyone knew it.

CHAPTER FOUR

The darkness rose around Frey, threatening to pull him under. He could still see the snake twisting around him, surrounding him with his massive body. Was this Apophis, like Ra thought? Whoever the snake was, maliciousness emanated from it, making Frey shiver. The snake wasn't going to help him fight away the darkness. The snake *was* darkness, and Frey wasn't strong or powerful enough to fight him.

The darkness swamped him. He screwed his eyes shut. He sucked in a breath, and his lungs filled with what felt like water.

He jerked awake, his body moving into a sitting position before he could think about what was happening. He was in his bedroom, in his house, and not in the darkness of the underworld.

Because that was what the darkness was, wasn't it? It was the Egyptian underworld, or at least the place where Apophis lived.

Frey sucked in a breath. His heart raced, and he told himself he didn't need to be afraid. He was home, nowhere near the underworld, and Apophis couldn't touch him.

He ran a hand through his long hair, pushing it away from his sweaty face. The visions were becoming stronger, and they came more often. He was used to dealing with them. He'd seen the future his entire life and had dealt with everything thrown at him.

He didn't understand why he now saw a god belonging to another pantheon. Maybe it was because Apophis threatened the entire world, not just the Norse pantheon. Maybe it was because of his closeness to Ra, but the visions had started before Ra had moved in with him, so he doubted it. Whatever the reason, it didn't matter. The only thing that did was that the visions were becoming worse, and Frey was afraid it meant that Apophis was becoming stronger.

He already knew he wouldn't be able to go back to sleep, so he got up and went to the bathroom. He was tempted just to wash his face, but his entire body felt sticky, so instead, he took off the clothes he'd slept in and took a shower. The hot water and familiar scent of his soap were soothing, and once he was done, he felt better, but still not well enough to go back to sleep.

He didn't have to sleep if he didn't want to, but living with humans, he'd started getting into the habit. Besides, a god's life was infinite. It was good to have periods of time in which he didn't have to do something or be bored. The visions also seemed easier to deal with when they occurred during his sleep, and as he left his bedroom, he wondered if that was what human dreaming felt like. His dreams had never been like this, and something told him humans didn't dream this way, either.

Ra had moved into one of Frey's guestrooms. There were two rooms, one smaller than the other, and Frey had been a bit embarrassed. Ra had seemed delighted, though, and he'd settled in easily, almost as if he'd always been part of Frey's life and had always lived in his home. To Frey's confusion, he felt better with Ra around. He'd tried telling himself it was because that way, he'd know someone was there for him when he had a vision, but that wasn't the truth. He felt more settled, as if he belonged more than before, which shouldn't have been possible.

But apparently, it was.

Gul was passed out in front of the fireplace, and he barely

looked up when Frey walked past him. Frey headed to the kitchen, poured himself a glass of water, then went to stand in front of the window to look out at the lake. It was dark, but knowing the lake was there helped him push his fears away. The visions were terrifying, and not knowing what would happen even more so, but Frey had faced many horrible things in his long life. Besides, he already knew when he'd die. The prophecy was clear that it would happen during Ragnarök, and Frey doubted Apophis had a hand in that. He wasn't supposed to, anyway.

"I thought I'd heard something," a soft voice said from behind Frey.

Frey wasn't startled, but he wasn't quite sure what to do with Ra. He turned to look at him, almost swallowing his tongue when he saw that Ra had gone to bed wearing only a pair of white flowing pants. Or maybe he slept naked and had thrown the pants on because he was coming out of the bedroom. Frey wasn't sure which image was worse — or better — and he firmly pushed both away.

"I'm sorry if I woke you up," he said.

"I've never slept much." Ra took a step forward. "Are you all right?"

"I am."

Ra came to stand next to Frey, and they both turned toward the lake. Frey was done drinking his water, but he clutched the glass. He still didn't know how to deal with Ra. His feelings for the other god were confusing. Ra was so powerful that Frey couldn't even imagine being like him, but he was also a man Frey found extremely attractive. He wanted Ra, but he also wasn't sure he could have him, considering everything.

"If you want to talk about what happened, I'll be happy to listen," Ra murmured, still not looking at Frey.

Frey was used to being on his own, and he enjoyed it. It

was nice not to have anyone to answer to and to be able to do whatever he wanted when he wanted it. But he was glad Ra was here tonight. His visions were becoming worse, but he still didn't have an explanation for them. He had no idea what to do with them or how to stop them—if he could.

"Just another vision," he explained. He didn't tell Ra about the darkness swamping him and making him feel like he was drowning.

Ra nodded. "I've had a feeling for a while now. It feels like something bad is about to happen, but I don't know what or even if there's something real about it. I hate feeling useless and powerless, but there's no way out."

"I feel the same."

And Frey could only imagine how it would feel if something happened and he hadn't done anything to stop it. Ra was right, though. How could they stop something they didn't know anything about? The only thing they were sure of was that a giant snake was involved, but was the snake Apophis, or was it someone else? Was the snake plotting something, or was there another person behind him, guiding him in the darkness?

No matter which way he looked, Frey didn't know what to do. He couldn't find answers, and he needed them.

Where was he supposed to find them?

Ra wanted to do more for Frey, but he wasn't sure there *was* anything he could do. Frey was the one having visions, having to deal with the darkness that surrounded Apophis. Ra couldn't help him by sharing his burden, but talking might help. It didn't usually help *him*, but Frey wasn't him.

They were as different as day and night, yet somehow, they fit together. Ra was convinced of that, and he was starting to wonder if maybe Frey felt the same. Now wasn't the time to bring that up, though. They were talking about Apophis and the visions, and that was what they should focus on.

"What are you thinking about?" He was always curious to know what was going on in Frey's mind.

"How guilty I'll feel if something happens and I haven't done anything to stop it."

"What can you do, though?"

"Right now, nothing, which I hate. But this is my world. Apophis can't have it."

"You could go back to Asgard." Ra had done some research into Frey, so he knew that was what the place where the Norse gods lived was called. There had to be a good reason for Frey to leave it behind, but it would still be the safest place for a Norse god if something happened to the human world.

But Frey shook his head. "I can't go back. Besides, I don't *want* to go back. The human world is my home now and will be for years to come."

Ra wasn't surprised. It seemed like things were just as complicated in the Norse pantheon as they were in the Egyptian one. "And you want the human world to be safe."

"It's not only for my benefit. Like you said, I could go back to Asgard, and I'll be just fine. What about all these humans, though?"

"Many gods would say they're not our problem."

Frey snorted. "And they'd be wrong. We created humans, right? It's our responsibility to keep an eye on them and ensure they're safe. They already have to deal with many awful things in their everyday lives. I won't abandon them to Apophis or whoever this giant asshole is."

"I agree."

Frey finally turned to look at Ra. "I would have thought you didn't care much. I know you don't have much contact with humans."

"I didn't until recently. That changed when two of my grandsons fell in love with humans, and of course, since I moved here. I don't fully understand the fascination some gods have with humans, and I don't know if I'll ever understand them, but I don't have to in order to want them to live. They don't have powers, but they're still beings who think, love, and die. They shouldn't have to deal with gods wanting to destroy them."

Ra could feel Frey's gaze on him, but he kept staring ahead. The sight of the lake was soothing, and he hadn't realized he needed that until now. His feelings were all over the place, both because of Apophis and because of Frey. Living with him was everything Ra could have hoped for, but he still needed more. He wanted Frey, but he wasn't sure Frey wanted him.

Frey sighed heavily. "This would be so much easier if we knew what's happening."

"It would be, but as it is, we have no way to know, which means we can't do anything." Ra hesitated, not wanting to remind Frey of bad things but needing to. "There were no differences in this vision?"

Frey shook his head. "It was as horrible as the others. The darkness feels like it's going to take over, like I'm drowning. The snake is there, not doing much of anything besides slithering around. I don't know what to think of this, but it can't be good."

"Not if Apophis is involved."

"That's what I was afraid of. What do we do if it's him?"

"We deal with it."

"It would be easier if we knew how to do that."

There were memories Ra didn't want to think about, and the fight with Apophis was one of those. It seemed he wouldn't be able to avoid the past for much longer, no matter how unwilling he was to face it. "I've restrained him to the underworld once. I'm sure I can do it again."

Frey was silent for a moment before asking, "But at what cost?"

"The cost doesn't matter. I'll do what I must to keep humanity and you safe."

"I can keep myself safe."

Ra didn't doubt that, but the need to protect Frey was strong. What was he protecting him from, though? Could he keep Frey safe when they didn't know what was happening?

"We need to do something about this," Ra said.

"But what? We don't know what's going on."

"I suspect someone is helping Apophis. He's powerful, but I'm not sure he's strong enough to create the storms and earthquakes from the underworld. He shouldn't be able to, which means someone is helping him, someone in the human world."

Frey considered that for a moment. "A human?"

Ra shook his head. "A human wouldn't even be able to stand being in front of him. They'd run away screaming. No, whoever this is, is a god, possibly a younger one who wasn't involved in the fight against Apophis the first time around. It's the only explanation I can think of for someone to be so stupid as to help him now."

"How do we find out the person helping him?"

"I can't tell you for sure, but maybe we should visit some of the places the natural disasters have impacted. There might be signs of whoever is helping Apophis, and maybe someone noticed them. We gods don't blend in easily."

That made the corner of Frey's lips curl. "I guess you have quite a bit of experience when it comes to that. I don't like the thought of staying home and doing nothing, so I guess this is the best we can do."

Ra liked that Frey included him. "We need to do some research, map out the disasters, and find out everything we can about them. This isn't going to be easy."

"Nothing worth fighting for ever is. I still want to do this."

"We'll do it." *Together.*

Ra didn't know what it would mean for the two of them, and he didn't want to worry about that right now. If Apophis was behind all of this, they'd have other things to worry about and focus on soon. The more they could find out about the disasters and who might be behind them, the better it would be. They had to be prepared for whatever was thrown at them next, be that Apophis or someone else.

But even with all that, Ra couldn't ignore the fact that he was terrified that something would happen to Frey. He shouldn't like the other god as much as he did, and not just because they'd only recently met. Frey belonged to another pantheon, which meant they couldn't be together.

Right?

As far as Ra knew, there had never been a relationship like this. What would stop him from trying, though? He was one of the most powerful gods in all pantheons, and he was sure he'd have Nu's support. Between the two of them, they could take on pretty much anyone.

Maybe even Apophis.

Chapter Five

R a watched the TV screen, feeling helpless and hating it. He was a god. Surely there had to be something he could do for the humans impacted by the massive storm.

But he couldn't think of anything. Even if he went there, he doubted they'd want his help. They'd be uncomfortable and awkward, and it would make things even worse.

He hadn't realized how hard being here while not being able to do anything would be. When he and Frey had decided to look into the disasters happening worldwide, he hadn't expected to feel anything for the people impacted. He did, and in a way he didn't understand and couldn't remember ever feeling. Before, humans had been something distant he barely thought about. Now he lived amongst them, and to his own surprise, he wanted to protect them. What was happening had to be because of a god — maybe Apophis — and Ra felt responsible.

"Things aren't going to get better if we don't do something," Frey murmured from his spot on the couch next to Ra.

"You told me to stay here when I wanted to go."

"I stand by that. You've seen how people in this town react to your presence. How do you think the people over there would? You being there would make things more awkward, and it's not something they can deal with at the moment. Trust me. We should stay back and try to find out who was behind all of this rather than go there and bother people who are already in trouble."

Ra understood the reasoning, but he needed to do

something. Sitting back and waiting for Apophis or whoever else was doing this to take the next step wouldn't help anyone, least of all the humans. "What do we do, then?"

Frey hummed as he thought. He did that often, and Ra had started to find it endearing. "How about we start investigating? We said we'd do it, but then this happened, and we've been spending all our time in front of the TV. If someone is going to stop this, it has to be us, and we won't be able to do that sitting on the couch."

Ra glared at him. "Isn't that what I've been saying?"

Frey smiled. "You were right, of course, and we do need to start doing something. Happy?"

"I won't be happy until all of this is over."

Frey huffed. "I get it. I might not be as impacted by all of this as you, but I want to protect humans. So, you're right. We should start investigating. Why don't we start with this disaster? It's the most recent."

"Which is why we shouldn't be heading there right now."

"What do we do, then?"

Ra had thought about it. He didn't often *stop* thinking about it, if he was honest. "Well, we both agreed that whoever the snake is, they're probably part of the Egyptian pantheon."

"It might be another, but I can't think of any snake god."

"But we know a snake god in the Egyptian pantheon. If the snake is Apophis, and if he found someone to help him, it'll be another Egyptian god. We should go there and at the very least talk to my parent. I'm sure they're keeping an eye on what's happening in the human world, and they'll want to know we're investigating."

"You always call them that."

Ra frowned. "Call them what?"

"Parent. Are we talking about your mother or your father?"

"Both. Nu is neither a woman nor a man, and they had me

on their own."

"Well, I'm glad you told me that before I met them. When should we go?"

Ra got up and turned off the TV. "We can go now. I doubt they have anything else to do since they keep complaining about being bored, and they'll be happy to see us."

Frey scrambled to follow Ra. "Maybe I should stay here. I can't exactly barge into a palace that belongs to another pantheon."

"Why not? Loki visits all the time."

Frey blinked. Once again, Ra was surprised at how much he wanted to drag Frey into his arms and kiss him. Frey was a perfectly competent god, but something in Ra wanted to protect him from what was happening. But for some reason, Frey was right in the middle of this, and there was nothing Ra could do to change that. The only thing he *could* do was stick by Frey and make sure to be there to protect him if he ever needed it.

"I'm not Loki," Frey eventually said.

Ra laughed. "I'm very much aware of that." And he was glad Frey was nothing like Loki. Ra liked Loki, but he was a lot to deal with. Frey was more understated, and Ra enjoyed spending time with him even when they watched TV and stayed silent. He couldn't imagine Loki being able to do that. The other god seemed to need to talk and fill the silence.

Frey looked down at himself and smoothed his sweater over his stomach. "Do I look okay?"

"You look perfect."

Frey rolled his eyes as if he thought it was a lie, but Ra would never lie to him. He thought Frey always looked perfect.

But they hadn't talked about whatever was happening between them, and Ra wasn't even sure something *was* happening. For now, it would be better to focus on the disasters and find out who was behind them. Maybe once all of this was over, they'd have time to get to know each other in a more personal way. Ra wasn't sure Frey wanted anything like that, but the more time he spent with the other god, the more *he* did. He couldn't believe he was the only one feeling that way, especially with how Frey looked at him sometimes.

"You'll have to guide me," Frey said. "I don't know where I'm going or how I should behave."

"Behave normally, as you would with your own family. Nu might be a god, but they are a good person. They like humans, which is why I believe they'll help us with this, especially if Apophis is involved." Ra still hoped that wasn't the case, but that hope became smaller and smaller every day. This was no coincidence.

He didn't give Frey time to obsess over what was about to happen. He took Frey's hand, smiling at his startled expression, and took them to the sky palace.

He'd started calling it that now, too, and he'd stopped telling himself not to. The palace didn't have a proper name, and sky palace was as good a name as any.

He landed them in front of Nu's door. That way, they wouldn't have to deal with anyone else. Nu wouldn't care about Frey's presence, but other gods might, and Ra wasn't up for a fight.

Frey looked down at himself once again as Ra knocked on the door. He smiled, trying to reassure Frey, but the door opened before he could tell him that he truly looked perfect and didn't have to worry about anything. Nu stood there, wearing large bright yellow large pants and an almost transparent tunic. They smiled at Ra, but their eyes widened when they caught sight of Frey.

"I know you," they said.

Frey's cheeks flushed. "We met when Loki was in trouble. I can go if my presence makes you uncomfortable."

Nu waved his words away. "Why would I be uncomfortable? Loki's friends are my friends, and besides, you're here with Ra." They looked from one to the other. "I'm tempted to ask what the two of you are doing together, but I suspect you're here for a different reason."

Ra sighed. He wished he could sit around, have tea, and talk about how Ra and Frey had met. It would be awkward, but it would be better than talking about the massive storm that had destroyed half a town in Germany.

"I'm sure you know about the storm."

Nu frowned. "How could I not? It's all over the news."

"We're here to talk about that. We suspect Apophis is involved and has help, probably from our pantheon."

Nu's expression had been grim when Ra had mentioned the storm, but now, it settled into something he didn't quite recognize.

Nu nodded. "I suspected these disasters weren't natural. We have a lot to talk about, and something tells me we don't have a lot of time to do so."

There wasn't much Frey could contribute to the conversation, so he spent most of the time watching Nu and Ra. He wasn't sure what he'd expected, but it wasn't what was in front of him. Nu was maternal and fussed over Ra as if he weren't a millennia-old powerful god. Most gods didn't care much about their children, although even in Frey's pantheon, sometimes things were different. He only had to think of Frigg and how she'd reacted when she lost her sons recently. Nu reminded Frey a bit of her, but they were more whimsical. They were serious now, though, as they and Ra talked about Apophis.

"Now, I know that these disasters seem ominous, but Apophis is in the underworld," Nu said.

It seemed they didn't want to believe Apophis was involved, just like Ra hadn't wanted to in the beginning. After hearing about Apophis, Frey hoped the snake god wasn't behind this, but what would be the odds?

Ra was already shaking his head. "It has to be him. It's not just about the disasters. Frey has visions, and he's been seeing a giant snake."

Nu's focus moved to Frey. He wished he could hide behind the couch he and Ra were sitting on, so he reminded himself that he was a god, too. He was nowhere near as powerful as Ra and Nu, and they could no doubt smite him with half a glance, but he wasn't powerless. Besides, everyone here was on the same side.

"And you believe someone is helping him?" Nu asked.

"Someone has to be. I checked, so I know Apophis is still imprisoned, but if he's behind all these disasters, someone is helping him. We need to find that someone and stop them. Hopefully, it'll be enough to send Apophis back to the deepest parts of the underworld."

Nu got to their feet. "Let's go, then."

Frey blinked. "Where are we going?" he asked as he got up.

"Since Ra believes one of our gods is involved, we should start talking to them."

"I doubt anyone will tell us if they were involved," he pointed out.

"I want to give whoever this is a chance to get out of the situation. They'll be punished, but they might be doing this because they believe they don't have a choice."

Frey highly doubted that, but this wasn't his pantheon. Even if it were, he wouldn't have a say in whatever punishment this person would face. "I should go back. This isn't my place, and I'm sure your people would talk to you more freely if I'm not here."

Ra stunned Frey when he took his hand. "Please. We're in this together, and you're the one having visions. You should be here with us."

Frey looked at Nu, expecting them to disagree, but they were already nodding. "We both want you here," they confirmed. "Besides, it's going to be fun watching everyone squirm at the thought of a god from another pantheon being here. They always grumble when Loki visits. I can't wait to find out how they feel about you."

Frey wasn't sure he liked being in this role, but he wanted to know what was happening.

To be honest, he wanted nothing to do with this entire situation, but unfortunately for him, he was right in the middle of it. He didn't have a choice. He would never forgive himself if he stepped away, ignored all of it, and humanity got hurt. Besides, Ra wouldn't be all right with that. He wanted to help, and the only way to do that was to find out what was happening.

So when Nu and Ra left Nu's wing of the palace, Frey went with them.

The palace wasn't something he was used to. All the Norse gods lived in Asgard, but they each had their own home. The Egyptian pantheon was different. Apparently, all the gods lived in the same palace, which was massive. It was so big it made even Frey feel small, which wasn't something he often experienced. It would have been easy for him to get lost, so he stuck as close to Ra and Nu as he could, happy that Ra hadn't let go of his hand. It was odd, but he enjoyed it.

"Who do we start with?" Ra asked.

"I was thinking Isis and Horus," Nu told him.

"I doubt they have anything to do with this. They have to remember what happened the last time Apophis was free. They wouldn't agree to help him."

"I hope you're right and that a minor god is involved, but

I still want to talk to them. Many gods go to them when they have a problem, so they might be aware of something I don't know."

Frey felt like a third wheel, but he continued following them until they reached a door. It didn't take long for a woman to answer after Nu knocked.

She was beautiful, with long black hair and dark skin. Her makeup was perfectly applied, and she wore a long dress that hugged her body. Her feet were bare, and as she looked at the three gods at her door, her expression grew worried.

"Nu. What are you doing here?"

"We need to talk to you and your son," Nu said, pushing past the woman and walking into the room beyond the door.

Ra pulled him along. Frey didn't miss the way the woman glanced at their hands, but what was he supposed to do? He wasn't in charge here, and if he'd tried to stay outside, Ra wouldn't have been happy.

The room they stepped into was wide and opened into a garden. From where they were, Frey could see a man sitting out there on a couch. He got to his feet when he heard them and came forward, possibly to welcome them, or to tell them to leave.

The man slightly bowed. He was as beautiful as the woman but looked younger, although that didn't mean much to gods. He only wore a white gown, and Frey had to work hard not to stare. Norse gods didn't usually walk around wearing only a gown, but he supposed they were used to snow and cold rather than the warmth of the Egyptian desert.

"Ra, Nu, welcome," the man said.

Ra nodded at him. "I apologize for bothering you, but we need to talk. This is Frey. He's a god from the Norse pantheon, and he's been having visions of a giant snake. Between that and the natural disasters, I'm afraid Apophis might be working on getting free."

Frey would have delivered the news differently, but Ra went straight to the point.

The woman gasped and raised a hand to her mouth. Frey suspected it was a calculated move from the way her gaze bounced around. She didn't look scared or shocked, more as if she'd expected what Ra had said.

Nu turned to Frey. "These are Isis and Horus."

Frey had researched the Egyptian pantheon after Ra had moved in with him, so he knew more or less who they were. They were powerful, so hopefully they'd be able to help.

"You can't be serious," Horus said. "Apophis has been stuck in the underworld for millennia. Who would help him get free?"

"Finding out is the reason we're here," Ra said. "Has anyone come to you complaining about something? Maybe they wanted advice or help?"

Isis shook her head. Horus was still thinking about it, but after a moment, he shook his head, too. Frey was disappointed but not surprised.

"You should talk to my father," Horus said. "He is the god of the underworld, after all. He might know more than we do, and at the very least, he's closer to Apophis than any of us."

Frey frowned as he tried to remember what he'd read about the Egyptian pantheon. Isis was married to Osiris, and Horus was their son. Something had happened between Osiris and his brother, and he'd ended up as the god of the underworld. Frey had thought that was Apophis, but Ra had told him Apophis wasn't quite a god.

"You should also talk to Set," Isis continued. "He helped defeat Apophis the first time. If something is happening, he needs to know."

Ra nodded. "He's next on our list. Please, if you hear anything, let us know."

"We will. Apophis coming back could kill all of us. We

can't stand for that."

Frey almost snorted. She hadn't mentioned humans, but he supposed that things in the Egyptian pantheon were very much like things in the Norse one. Gods seldom cared about anyone but themselves, especially not humans.

They left soon after, since Isis and Horus didn't know anything. Once outside, they looked at each other, and Ra sighed. "I suppose we should visit Set and find out if he'll be eager to help this time around, too."

Frey moved closer and leaned against Ra. He wanted him to know that even if this other god said no, Ra wouldn't fight Apophis alone. Frey might not be able to do much, but whatever he *could* do, he would, even if it meant sacrificing himself for the good of humanity.

Since they were already at the palace, Ra guided Nu and Frey to Set's apartments. They were smaller, but it had never bothered him, or at least, Ra thought not.

"Who's Set?" Frey asked as they walked.

Like all gods, Set wasn't easy to deal with. He'd done things Ra found abhorrent, but he'd also been by Ra's side when Ra needed him. "It's complicated," Ra said.

Frey snorted. "When isn't something complicated when it comes to gods? You don't have to tell me if you don't want to, but I'd like to know who I'm about to face."

"He's Isis and Osiris's brother," Nu explained. "To make a long story short, he and Osiris fought, and Set killed his brother. Isis brought Osiris back to life, in a way. He wasn't the same, which is how he became the god of the underworld."

"But it's been a long time since this happened," Ra rushed to say. "Even though Set is a god of chaos and disorder, he helped me the last time I faced Apophis."

"He kind of sounds *like* Apophis," Frey said.

"He shares some of Apophis's characteristics. Like I said, he's the god of chaos and disorder, but also of storms and darkness. Apophis revels in those things, but Set was the most powerful god on my barrage against Apophis, right after me. We wouldn't have managed to subdue Apophis if it weren't for him." Ra hesitated. "But Set can be difficult. He's a contradiction, and while I do believe he will help us in the end, he might make us work for it."

"At least we'll know he's on our side. We need more allies."

"What about your pantheon?" Nu asked.

Ra didn't know why Frey had left his pantheon and Asgard behind, but he suspected it was nothing good. They hadn't talked about it, and he could see that Frey was uncomfortable. He was glad they'd reached Set's wing of the palace, and he quickly knocked on the main door. That got Nu's attention, and Ra couldn't ignore the way Frey's shoulders relaxed.

He stepped closer, pulling Frey against his side. "All right?"

Frey nodded. "This is a lot, but I'll be fine."

A servant opened the door. Her eyes widened when she saw who was there, and she quickly let them in, then disappeared deeper into the wing, no doubt telling Set they were there. Ra took a moment to focus on Frey, ensuring the other god was truly all right. He wished they could have some time on their own, but that would come later, once they were done with this conversation. This would be it for today. They'd have to come back and talk to more gods, but unfortunately, there were hundreds of them. It would be impossible to talk to all of them before Apophis did whatever he was planning, but Ra couldn't think of another way to find out who was helping him.

"To what do I owe this pleasure?" Set asked as he strode

into the room.

Ra didn't miss the fact that they hadn't been asked to come deeper into the wing. Set was keeping them at arm's length, but that wasn't a surprise.

He nodded at Set. "You haven't changed a bit," he commented.

Set wore different clothes from the last time they'd seen each other, but then, it had been hundreds of years. He seemed to enjoy the same kind of style Ra did, because he was wearing a suit with a shirt open at the collar. The suit was black, and the shirt was white, which looked pleasing against Set's skin. Set's fingers were adorned with golden rings, but that was all the jewelry Ra could see.

Set's gaze stopped on Frey, and Ra had to resist the urge to push Frey behind himself. Set wasn't a danger, but Apophis definitely would be.

"We suspect Apophis is coming back," Nu said, going straight to the point like Ra had with Isis and Horus. "We need to know if we can count on you to help this time around, too."

Set didn't look surprised. "The storms and earthquakes."

"Yes," Ra agreed. "It has to be Apophis, or at the very least, someone related to him. You know what he wants and what will happen if we don't intervene."

Set crossed his arms over his chest. "So you want me to do the same as last time?"

"When I face him, I'd like for you to be by my side, yes."

"And what will I gain from that?"

Ra wasn't surprised at the question. "You'll save humanity. Isn't that enough?"

Set laughed. "It is. I quite enjoy the human world. Life would be boring without it and the humans who inhabit it. I'll be by your side when you fight Apophis."

Now *that* was a surprise. Ra hadn't expected Set to agree

so readily. He wasn't quite sure what to say or how to behave. Nu didn't seem to have that problem, though.

"Thank you," they said. "I knew we could count on you."

"I'm not doing this for you. I'm doing it because I like humans more than gods." Set's gaze stopped on Frey. "Although if all gods were as pretty as he is, maybe that would be different."

Ra glared at Set, who seemed to find it amusing. "Was there anything else you wanted?" he asked.

Ra forced himself to relax. They had what they'd come for. Set would help, which was all that mattered. "No. Thank you for this."

"As I said, I'm not doing it for you. You know where the door is. When you need me, call me, and I'll be there."

He turned around, leaving the three of them there with the servant, who hovered by the door. It was almost as if she was afraid they'd refuse to leave, so Ra pulled Frey toward her again. "Thank you," he said as they left.

She looked startled and nodded before closing the door.

"That went better than I expected," Nu said.

"He could have been much more difficult," Ra agreed. "I don't think I have it in me to deal with any more gods today."

Nu's eyes glittered. "Does that go for all gods, or do you make exceptions? Because I'm sure Frey would enjoy spending time with you in my private garden."

Ra almost groaned. There was no way Frey couldn't see what Nu was doing. They were playing matchmaker, and Ra should have expected it.

He didn't mind. He *wanted* to be matched with Frey, but he wasn't willing to push the other god around to get that.

But Frey was smiling and nodding. "I think I would like that. I love Finland, but I've never been to Egypt."

"The palace isn't Egypt," Ra warned him.

"But my gardens are beautiful," Nu intervened. "I'll have

someone bring you food, and you can have a picnic or talk. It would be great if you could find a better topic of conversation than Apophis, but I won't hold my breath."

Frey laughed. "It does seem like Apophis has become central to our lives."

"Considering what he's doing, it's not surprising," Ra said.

Nu's expression turned almost sad. "Not surprising, but there's more to life than fighting with Apophis. I wish you didn't have to do it again."

"I wish the same, but it is what it is." Ra looked at Frey, who was still beside him. "We'll take that offer of visiting the gardens, though. I'm sure Frey can do with some relaxation after the conversation we had."

Nu's smile was smug. "I'll be in my wing if you need me, but I'd rather you don't need me. I need rest. I'm not young anymore, after all."

Ra almost rolled his eyes. "You'll outlive all of us."

Nu patted his arm. "I sure hope that won't be the case."

Ra hoped no one would die at all, but he knew better. If Apophis was behind all of this, he wanted revenge for what Ra and the others had done to him the first time he'd tried taking over the human world. He'd come for Ra, Set, and everyone else, and he wouldn't stop until he got what he wanted.

All of them dead, and him in absolute power.

Ra was still thinking about that as he led Frey toward Nu's apartment. Once they got there, Nu disappeared deeper into their wing while Ra pulled Frey toward the open door that opened into the garden. "Ready to relax?" he asked.

Frey nodded. "I'll be happy to stop thinking about Apophis for a few hours." He hesitated. "But I want you to know that you won't be alone facing Apophis. I know he's dangerous and that he'll probably kill me without a second thought, but even if none of your gods agree to help beyond Set, I'll be there, and I won't be the only one."

Ra didn't know what to say to that. "Thank you."

"Don't thank me yet. We might lose, and the human world will be in trouble. I know all of us will do our best to help you, though."

It might not be enough, and they might lose everything, including their lives, but it felt good to realize Ra wasn't alone. Whatever happened, Frey would be by his side, along with the rest of Frey's family. It might not be his blood family, at least not entirely, but he couldn't find it in himself to care.

Frey was more than ready to stop obsessing over Apophis for a few hours, so he eagerly followed Ra toward the open door that led to the gardens. He hadn't seen much of them before, but he'd noticed how beautiful what he could see was. Exploring the rest sounded like a good distraction, although he couldn't help but worry about what it would mean for him and Ra.

Frey had no idea what to do with the other god. He felt closer to him than he'd been to most people, but not the same way he was close to Loki or his sister. Did that mean something? And what about the handholding? What had Ra been thinking?

He hadn't seemed to care that Nu could see them or that Isis, Horus, or Set had. He'd held Frey's hand the entire time, and he still was.

Ra pulled Frey down the path that led away from the terrace.

Frey didn't know where to look, but most of his attention was on Ra rather than on the plants.

"Nu spends most of their time here," Ra explained. "They love it, and I agree that it's lovely."

"What about you? How much time do you spend in this garden?"

"Not as much as I wish I could."

"You don't have to stay in Finland if you'd rather be here," Frey pointed out, slightly wounded.

But Ra shook his head. "That's not what I meant. Even when I lived in the palace, I stayed in my wing, away from all the other gods, including Nu."

"Why? It's clear they care about you." Enough to try to get Ra and Frey together. Frey might not know them well, but even he had been able to see that was what they were doing when they'd told Ra to take Frey to the garden.

"And I care about them. Something happened long ago, though, and I decided to retire. I felt it was best for everyone if I stayed away."

"Do you want to talk about it?"

Ra shrugged. "Not particularly, but maybe I should." He hesitated. "Thousands of years ago, I wasn't the same person I am now. I was angry with humans and the way they behaved, and I created a goddess to destroy them. I changed my mind and managed to stop her, but it was clear to me then that I had to step away. I was dangerous, and I needed to find myself again."

Frey could understand. He might not have been through whatever Ra was talking about, but some days, he wasn't happy with the way he thought or even behaved. All gods changed during the infinite life they lived. It was good that Ra had realized what was happening and put a stop to it, and even better, he'd decided to do something about it.

"But you've come out of retirement."

"It was time. There's no one better to take on Apophis, and I'm not the same person I was before. It was a lack of judgment on my part, and I won't do that again. I believe that spending more time with humans will help." He looked sideways at Frey. "Just like spending more time with you is helping."

What was Frey supposed to say to that? "I'm not doing anything."

"You don't even realize it, but you anchor me in a way no one else ever has." Ra's hand tightened around Frey's. "We haven't talked about it, but maybe it's time to do so."

Frey had been hoping to avoid this conversation for a while longer. "Wouldn't it be best if we focused on Apophis and what's happening there?"

Ra's lips curled into a smile. "Maybe, but you do realize why Nu sent us here in the gardens, right? Besides, you agreed to stop thinking about Apophis for a while."

Frey sighed. All of that was true. "I do want to enjoy some time without obsessing over all of this."

"As do I. We can walk or do whatever you want."

That gave Frey pause. "*Whatever* I want?"

Ra looked puzzled but nodded. "Within reason."

Frey grinned and stepped away from Ra. Gul was going to love this place.

He summoned the boar, who appeared in front of him. Gul squinted as he looked around, then bounced over to Frey when he saw him. Frey laughed and gave Gul's head a good scratch before turning back to Ra. "How about we go for a ride?"

Ra eyed the boar. "On him?"

Ra and Gul had been getting to know each other now that Ra lived with Frey, but it was clear Ra was still hesitant. "He won't hurt you. I ride him when I have the chance, but in the human world, I try not to because I don't want to scare the humans. Here, we're free to do that."

Ra still didn't look convinced. "If you insist," he said eventually, surprising Frey.

"I don't," Frey told him. "You don't have to do anything you don't want to. I just thought it would be fun for Gul and us. He doesn't get to run around a lot."

Ra sighed. "Just show me what I'm supposed to do."

Frey was grinning like a loon as he helped Ra climb on top of Gul's back. "Have you ever ridden a horse?" he asked as he settled behind Ra.

"A horse, yes. Not a boar."

"Remember that he's intelligent, much more than an animal. He understands what we say, and he knows you're wary. Just talk to him like you talk to me."

Ra looked over his shoulder. It felt odd for Frey to be behind him, because Ra was so much taller. It would be safer for Ra to be in front, though. "I'd much rather talk to you."

The words went straight to Frey's heart. "We can talk as much as we want later. Unless you'd rather not do this?"

Ra shook his head. "Show me how you have fun."

So Frey did. He gently pushed his heels into Gul's sides, and Gul jumped forward. Ra yelped and grabbed one of Frey's hands. Frey had the other on Gul's neck, but he wrapped the arm Ra was holding around Ra's waist to hold him close.

"You're safe," he whispered. It felt foolish, considering who Ra was, but even though Frey was nowhere near as powerful as Ra, it didn't mean he didn't want to keep the other god safe. It didn't make sense, but then, love seldom did.

And Frey was falling in love with Ra.

He'd felt it happening, but he hadn't been able to stop it and stopped trying. Whatever happened, it seemed like Ra felt similarly, or at the very least, that he was headed that way. They'd need to talk about it, but Frey focused on the moment and how Ra felt against him, snuggled into his arms for now.

There was no way to know what would happen with Apophis and what the future held for Frey and Ra, but Frey knew he wanted their futures to be intertwined. He'd already been planning on doing everything he could to keep Ra safe, but that feeling had grown, and he felt even more deeply about it now.

Gul ran through the gardens, chasing butterflies and birds. When he finally slowed down, Ra had stopped clutching at Frey's arm as if he were terrified of falling, and he turned to look at him. He was smiling and looked younger than he ever had since Frey had met him. Doing this had been a good idea.

Frey couldn't look away. He leaned closer, and Ra mirrored his movement. Their lips were close enough to kiss. Frey's heart raced, and he pressed even closer, but Gul started running again just then. Ra yelped and turned to grab Gul's fur. The boar wasn't finished running, and Frey couldn't blame him, even though it had interrupted his first kiss with Ra.

They'd have other opportunities. Frey would make sure of it.

CHAPTER SIX

They kept the TV on all the time when they were awake now so they could find out if something happened. Ra didn't like it, but they didn't have a choice. If something else happened and they managed to get there on time, they might be able to find out who was helping Apophis. It was grim to have to listen to the news constantly, and when he could, he tried to stay away from the living room. That meant he was spending less time with Frey, who was hooked on the news and spent most of his days on the couch. Ra wished he didn't, but he understood the need for Frey to keep an eye on the news, just like he understood his own need for a break.

He'd already dealt with Apophis once. He knew how dire things would become if Apophis came back. He didn't have to see it, and he already knew all about it. Thankfully, Frey seemed to understand, but whatever progress they'd been making between them had stopped.

"Ra?" Frey called from the living room.

Ra was in the kitchen, putting together a sandwich. For now, that was all he could manage for lunch, but he'd promised himself he'd take cooking lessons. He could easily use his powers to get food, but a part of him wanted to impress Frey with how good he was getting at acting human. There was no hiding that he wasn't one of them, but he could stop behaving like he had no idea what was happening around him, even though that was how he felt most of the time.

"Lunch is almost ready," Ra called back.

"You need to come here. Now."

The tension in Frey's voice was enough to spur Ra to set down the knife he'd been using to spread mayo on the bread. He rushed to the living room, wondering if something had happened to Frey, but Frey was on the couch, exactly like he had been when Ra had walked past him ten minutes ago.

He wore a soft pair of pants, a thick sweater, and no socks. He'd been bundled in a blanket, but he'd pushed it away and was now leaning forward, his attention on the screen.

Ra didn't need to ask what had happened to know. He swallowed and looked at the screen, the images flooding his mind as he watched.

It was an earthquake. The images jumped from showing a tiny town somewhere with crumbling palaces and houses and people running in the dusty street to cameras inside buildings. All of the images had one thing in common — everything was shaking.

Frey looked at Ra for a few seconds before turning his attention back to the TV. "It's a bad one," he said.

Ra nodded and sat on the arm of the couch. Now that he'd started watching, he couldn't look away. "How many casualties?"

"They don't know yet. It lasted for *minutes*, Ra. Do you know how long that is when there's an earthquake?"

"When did it happen?"

"Just a few minutes ago. It's breaking news, so there's no way to know how many people got hurt."

"Where?" Ra didn't recognize the images, but he wasn't very familiar with the human world.

"The alps."

"I wasn't aware they were a seismic area."

"They weren't until now."

So this wasn't natural. Ra had expected that, but seeing proof made him queasy. He'd still been hoping Apophis had nothing to do with any of this, but he'd known it was wishful thinking. Natural disasters and chaos were Apophis's brand and signature, and there was no denying his involvement.

"Is there anything we can do?" If there was, Ra wanted to do it. Going there might create even more chaos, but he and Frey could help the humans impacted by this earthquake.

Ra felt responsible, even though Apophis was the only one who truly was. But Ra's job was to keep an eye on his pantheon and ensure they didn't hurt humans, and he'd failed spectacularly.

Except it wasn't his job anymore. He'd retired, leaving the gods to do what they wanted. Most of them were harmless, and as far as he knew, nothing major had happened in hundreds of years. Besides, Apophis wasn't part of the pantheon. He wasn't technically a god, either. He was a giant snake, older than many things in the world, possibly even Ra.

And Ra would have to deal with him.

Frey got to his feet, startling Ra.

"What are you doing?" Ra asked.

Frey pointed at the TV. "We have to do something. I told you we needed to stay away last time, but they need our help. Besides, if we go there now, we might be able to find out more about what happened. Maybe someone noticed something. Maybe the god helping Apophis is still there."

It would be stupid, but Ra nodded anyway. He'd just been thinking he wanted to help, and Frey was offering him the option to do so. He wasn't about to refuse and stay home.

"Let's go."

With only a thought, Ra changed the clothes he was wearing. In the house, he stayed away from suits and shirts, wearing soft pants like Frey and sweaters that kept him warm. They wouldn't do in an earthquake situation, so he chose something sturdier, including a pair of boots on his feet. He reached up to braid his hair as Frey changed, for once not going to the bedroom to do so. Frey tended not to use his powers much, something that intrigued Ra, but thankfully, it was clear he didn't want to waste time today.

"Ready when you are," Frey declared as he put up his hair in a bun.

Ra nodded and turned back to the TV. It was easy enough to wait for the name of the area impacted, but since it was vast, he grabbed Frey's hand so they wouldn't be separated. Frey's eyes widened, but the next second, they were gone and appearing in the alps.

Ra had chosen one of the worst impacted areas. The building to his right had been pretty once. The outside wall was yellow, and every balcony had flowers hanging from it. The part closest to Ra was intact, but just a little ahead, it had crumbled down. People were digging into the rubble, and without thinking about it, Ra moved toward them.

"Is there someone in there?"

The man next to him was startled and took a step back, almost falling. Ra caught him and kept him on his feet, staring at him and waiting for him to answer. When he didn't, Ra turned to the other men digging. "Are there people under here?" he asked.

One of the men nodded. His face was dirty with dust and blood that trickled slowly from his forehead. "My wife and daughter."

Ra nodded and turned his attention to the building. He closed his eyes, using his mind to look for the humans. They could very well be dead, but he hoped that wouldn't be the case for the man's sake.

Everyone around him was looking for survivors, people who might be stuck under the crumbling houses. Ra had lived through several earthquakes, so he knew they might not find many people alive, especially without help. It would take them days to dig, and the survivors would be dead by then.

Luckily, Ra and Frey were here.

Ra located two heartbeats. One was stronger than the other, and he focused on that one, raising his hands. He opened his eyes as he used his powers to raise the rubble in the area where the heartbeats were located. Someone next to him gasped, but he didn't turn to look at who it was or why they were doing so.

"Go," he ordered.

The man dove into the ruins of the house that had been his home. He disappeared from sight, and Ra focused more of his power on holding half of the house in the air. He could do so for hours, but he wanted to help more people, which meant he couldn't tire himself out.

The other men finally moved, going after the first one to help. The first man eventually came out, carrying a little girl that was covered in dust that had turned her hair a dark gray. The man didn't look at Ra, but Ra didn't need a thank you. He was doing this because it was the right thing to do, not because he was looking to be thanked.

The other men finally appeared, two of them holding up a woman between them. Another ran ahead, possibly looking for a doctor. He was talking in a language Ra didn't understand, but Ra didn't *need* to understand.

"Anyone else in there?" he asked.

The men looked at him, confused. They probably didn't understand him, which could be a problem. Since Ra didn't want to be doing this for nothing, he focused on the house, looking for another heartbeat. He couldn't hear anything, so he slowly lowered the rubble.

Then he moved on to the next problem.

Frey didn't know where to start. He wanted to help everyone, but he was only one man. Well, one god, but he wasn't that powerful. Still, he was doing everything he could, helping humans dig into the houses that had come down and guiding wounded people toward the tents that served as an infirmary. Ra was doing a much more important job, raising rubble and helping people get out from under it. Frey was in awe. He didn't have the power to do the same, but maybe he didn't need it. He was helping in his own way, and that was enough.

He guided an elderly woman toward a chair, helping her sit down before looking around for a bottle of water. Her clothes were covered in dirt, and she had a cut on her cheek. She'd been crying, the tears digging tracks into the thick dust on her face.

Frey crouched next to her and handed her the water. "Do you need anything else?"

He'd quickly realized he'd need to speak Italian if he wanted the people here to understand him. Luckily, he'd made a point of learning as many languages as he could over the years. There wasn't much else he could do as a god, and it came in handy now.

The lady shook her head. "Thank you," she said in a trembling voice.

Frey had found her leaning against an orange house that had possibly been hers once. She'd been trying to get in, but she was tired and breathless. Frey suspected part of that was due to the dust in the air.

"You need to stay here," he said. "You can't go into your house. It could come down on your head."

"Maybe it should," she murmured. "I don't have anything left."

Frey's heart broke for her, but there was little he could do to help her beyond what he was already doing. He patted her hand, hoping to give her even just a bit of comfort. "I know things look dire now, but you're alive. That's what matters."

She looked at him, and he reacted without thinking, reaching out to dry a new tear that rolled down her face. She blinked, clearly surprised.

"Why are you doing this?"

"Because you need help."

"But you're not our god. None of them are here."

Frey didn't know much about the Roman pantheon, but it was true none of its gods were here. "It doesn't matter who I am. You need help, and I can provide it." He hesitated. He didn't want to hurt her more than she already was, but he hadn't yet had the chance to ask people if they'd seen anything. "Can I ask you a few questions?"

She turned to look at her house, then back at Frey, and nodded. "You can ask me anything. You saved my life."

Frey wouldn't go that far. "Have you seen anything strange lately? Maybe people who don't belong here? Is there anything you can think of that was out of place before the earthquake."

The woman frowned. "Why are you asking that?"

Frey should have known that the people he asked questions to would want answers. He wasn't sure what to tell them. He didn't want to freak people out even more than they already were. Still, she might not tell him what she knew if he didn't at least hint at what he was aiming for. "We think the earthquake might not have been natural."

Her eyes widened, and she leaned back. "A god?"

"Possibly."

She spat on the ground, starting Frey. "All gods are assholes. They take and take, not caring one bit about us humans." She looked at Frey. "Except you. You're good."

"I don't know if I am, but did you see anything?"

"A lion."

That wasn't what Frey had expected. "As in the big cat?"

She nodded. "I saw it several times, and I'm not the only one. He was roaming up the mountain."

"Did you tell anyone?"

"We did, but they didn't believe us. They told us we were dreaming or imagining things. It was real, though, right?"

"I believe so. Will you be okay here?"

She waved him away. "I'm safe, thanks to you."

Frey stayed for a moment longer, just enough time for her to tell him where the lion had been seen. It wasn't far, but it was up the mountain. Frey wondered if Ra would want to come along or if he'd rather stay here to help, but he wasn't sure. It was better to talk to Ra and have him explain what he wanted to do, so Frey went to find him.

He was raising rubble again, a group of people rushing into the destroyed house to grab the survivors under it. They seemed to have found a rhythm now, and within minutes, the humans were dragging out three people, one of them a child. Ra waited a moment longer, and then he slowly lowered the rubble until it crashed back on what had once been a house.

Ra turned, probably headed to the next house, but his gaze caught with Frey's. They stared at each other for a moment. They had to be a sight, both of them dirty and sweating, but Frey didn't care. Ra was the most beautiful man he'd ever seen, even more beautiful because of how kind he was. Any other god would have stayed away from this place. Hell, all the other gods *had* stayed away. Frey and Ra were the only ones here.

But they *were* here, and they were helping.

"Is everything all right?" Ra asked as he moved closer.

Frey shook off the thoughts about Ra and focused on the situation at hand. "I was talking to a woman who said she saw a lion up the mountain. She wasn't the only one, but no one believed them."

Ra frowned. "You think it was Apophis's helper?"

"Why else would a lion roam the mountains in Italy?"

Ra looked around. "We should go check."

"I know you want to stay." Frey reached out to take one of

Ra's hands. "I do, too. But if this person is still around, we'll keep these people safe by tracking them. We can come back as soon as we find out everything we can about this lion."

Ra turned his attention back to Frey. "You're right. Besides, our job is to find the *helper* and stop Apophis. If we don't, the situation will be much worse."

But it was obvious he was hesitant to leave the humans. There could still be survivors under the rubble, people who wouldn't live for long if no one helped them as soon as possible.

Frey had promised Ra he wouldn't do this alone, and he'd meant it. He hadn't just been talking about Apophis, though.

He took out his phone. "I'm calling Loki."

Ra frowned. "Why?"

"He can contact the others, and they can all come here. These people need help, and while I know gods don't usually get mixed up in these things, I can't stay back and do nothing. You and I need to go, but we're not the only ones who can help."

Ra reached for Frey before Frey could react. He pulled Frey closer, and when Frey realized what was happening, his eyes widened. He didn't push away from Ra as Ra kissed him. If anything, he leaned closer, eager to deepen the kiss.

But now wasn't the time, and this wasn't the place. Loki answered the call, and Frey took a step back. He kept a hand on Ra's chest as he explained to Loki what had happened and what they needed. Loki promised to be there soon as possible and to call everyone he could think of who would help, which was a relief.

As soon as Frey hung up, he and Ra left. The woman had given Frey a pretty good description of the area where she'd seen the lion, so that was where he headed. This time, he was the one holding Ra's hand, and when they appeared at the spot where the lion had been seen, Ra didn't let go.

Frey looked around. The only thing he could see were trees, trees, and more trees. There was a path a short distance away, and it looked well-maintained. The woman had mentioned she'd been on the mountain to take a walk, so this was probably where she'd been walking.

Frey wanted to ride Gul, but there was no way to know what they'd find. He wouldn't risk his boar.

"Where do we start?" Ra asked.

"We should walk around and see if we can find anything. Can you think of anyone who can change into a lion?"

Ra pulled Frey along, never letting go of him. Frey was grateful because he wasn't athletic, but Ra helped and kept him on his feet.

"I can think of a few gods," Ra said. He sounded distracted. "Sekmet, for one. She and I have a complicated relationship, so it could be her." He hesitated. "She's the god I created to destroy humanity."

"And you think she decided to finish the job?"

"I don't, and she's not the only god who can turn into a lion. The lady said lion and not lioness?"

"Yeah, but most people would probably call a lioness a lion."

No matter how long they poked around, they didn't find much. They found footprints that pointed to a lion, like the lady had said, but that was all. They had more information now, but would it be enough? They needed to find out who was behind this and stop them. If that meant they'd have to investigate every god who could turn into a lion, they'd do it.

But first, they'd head back to town and help some more.

CHAPTER SEVEN

The sound of breaking news on the TV made Ra groan. It couldn't be good, and even though he wanted nothing less than to raise the volume, he did. Whatever had happened, he and Frey needed to know.

" . . . the water is rising quickly and steadily," the woman on the screen said. "Several neighborhoods are already underwater, and while the authorities are working hard to ensure that no one is left behind, the situation is desperate."

Ra leaned forward. He tried to get every detail as to where this was happening so he and Frey could go. They needed to know everything they could find out before arriving, but they had to leave quickly.

"Another one?" Frey asked as he walked into the living room. He was already wearing sturdy boots and cargo pants.

Ra got to his feet and nodded. "A flood this time. Ready to go?"

Frey appeared determined, but Ra didn't miss the fear in his gaze. "Ready when you are."

It only took seconds for Ra to change into more appropriate clothing, then to take Frey's hand and move them to the flooded area.

As soon as they got there, they were drenched. It was heavily raining, and everywhere Ra looked, there was water. It was quickly rising, just like the woman on TV had said, and he could see that if they stayed where they were, it wouldn't take long for the water to be up to their ankles.

Frey pushed his wet hair away from his face. "Where

would they be if they're responsible for this?"

Ra looked around. "There," he said, pointing at an area of town that was higher than the rest. Whoever was behind this would have a good view of the town going underwater from there.

Frey nodded and disappeared. Ra quickly followed, even though he was eager to help the humans. First, they needed to make sure the person responsible for this was gone. It would be too dangerous for whatever human they saved if Apophis's ally was still around.

It was raining even harder here. It was almost impossible for Ra to see anything, and he glared at the sky. "I'll take care of the rain," he said.

Frey nodded. "It'll be easier for us to find clues if it's not raining, but be careful."

Ra snorted. "I'm the sun god."

He raised his hands to the sky and closed his eyes. The sun was there but hidden behind the clouds and rain. All Ra had to do was to nudge them aside so the sun could shine again. In seconds, he felt warmth on his skin, and when he opened his eyes, it was to find that the clouds were dissipating and the sun was peeking out.

Frey nodded at him. "Good job."

No one else would have said that to Ra. They'd have been too afraid to say the obvious, but Frey wasn't. He wanted Ra to know how he felt about what they were doing, and Ra liked that.

They poked around for a bit, but with the water that had come down, they couldn't find anything, not even footprints. Frey disappeared between a bunch of trees, but Ra didn't get worried until he didn't come back for several minutes. Then he followed Frey, eager to find out where the other god was.

He found Frey at the entrance of a cave. Everything was wet and slippery, and Frey carefully climbed down some rocks to get inside the cave.

"What are you doing?" Ra asked.

Frey didn't even look at him. "I think the person who was here might have visited the cave."

"Why do you think that?"

"Wouldn't you have once it started raining?"

That wasn't the worst idea Ra had ever heard. "I don't want you to get hurt."

Frey waved Ra's words away without even looking at him. "I'll be fine. Why don't you come with me?"

Ra had no intention of staying back if Frey went inside. He followed, careful not to slip and hurt himself. It would be easier to simply appear wherever they were going, but without knowing what they'd find inside, it was safer for both of them to do this the human way.

It wasn't easy, but thankfully, the humans had placed railings in the cave. Ra had to grab them a few times so he wouldn't fall on his face, but finally, he stood next to Frey, and both of them were peering deeper into the cave.

"How deep would they have gone?" Ra asked. They could go deeper, but he wasn't looking forward to it. It was dark and smelled foul.

Frey shrugged. "I don't know. I wouldn't have gone too far, but I'm not an evil mastermind."

"That would be Apophis," Ra murmured. He took a step forward, wondering if they could find anything in the darkness and water. It didn't feel like it, but maybe they'd be lucky.

They were. Ra had only taken a few steps forward before the sulfur smell caught his attention. He squinted but couldn't see anything, which meant he had a decision to make. He could use his powers and draw the attention of whoever might be here, or he could stay in the darkness and not know what he'd found.

"I don't think anyone is here," Frey murmured. "If they were, they'd already have killed us."

Ra took that as a go-ahead, and, raising a hand, he lit it with the power of the sun.

Light bounced off the walls of the cave. Ra didn't look around, knowing Frey would protect him if someone was there. Instead, he crouched next to the area where he'd smelled sulfur and looked.

The ground was primarily made of rocks and mud. On one of the rocks, he could see signs of scorching, which went hand in hand with the sulfur. He rubbed his fingertips on the stone, and they came back dirty with soot.

"What is that?" Frey asked.

"Sulfur. Demons." It was one of the things Ra had been afraid of.

"And footprints," Frey said, pointing next to the stone.

Ra could see what was left of a print belonging to a big cat. In front of it was a shoe print, which meant the god had shifted to their human form. It would be the only way for them to summon the demons.

Ra got back to his feet. "Between the lion and the demons, this has to be an Egyptian god," he declared.

Frey didn't look surprised. "I'm sorry."

"Don't be. You have nothing to do with this, and it was my fault. I should have been more careful. Instead of isolating myself, not wanting to know anything about the other gods, I should have kept an eye on them."

Frey put a hand on Ra's arm. "Even if you had, you wouldn't have known about this. They're hiding, which means they don't want to face you, at least not yet."

"But I might have been able to stop them before they started this madness."

"I doubt that. If they truly want Apophis to be free, it means they want something. Probably more power, which isn't something you could have given them. They'd have re-belled against you anyway."

Ra looked around but couldn't see anything that would lead him to the god behind all of this. He hoped it was a minor god, someone less powerful, but that wouldn't help him if they managed to free Apophis. *He* was the dangerous one, the one creating the disasters and bringing so much pain to the human world. The lion was helping, summoning demons, but they weren't responsible.

That didn't mean they weren't dangerous. Ra had no doubt they were and that they'd have to take care of this lion before they could get to Apophis. If they were lucky, the lion's absence would mean Apophis would once again be stuck in the underworld.

But Ra had already been extremely lucky, and he wasn't sure that luck would hold for much longer.

Frey hated this cave and wanted out, but first they had to be sure they hadn't missed anything. They still didn't have any more clues as to who the lion was, and it was starting to worry him.

He peeked at Ra, who was focused on the stone. Ra seemed convinced this was an Egyptian god, and Frey agreed. Considering they were talking about Apophis, it would make sense that an Egyptian god was trying to free him. He was worried about how Ra would react once they found out who it was. Would Ra get angry and destroy the god, or would he be unable to do so because of what they meant to him?

Even not knowing who was behind all of this, Frey could see how much Ra cared. He wouldn't take it well if this was a god with whom he didn't have much contact, but it would be even worse if it was someone important to him.

Unfortunately, there was no way to find out. They'd made

a list of who could change into a lion, but there were too many options.

Frey sighed heavily. "We'll need to talk to everyone," he said.

Ra was still distracted, but he nodded. "I agree. At this point, it's the only way we have to find out who's behind this."

"I doubt they'll tell us to our faces that it's them."

"I like to think I'll know, but there's no way for me to be sure. I don't like this, Frey."

Frey knew how Ra felt. "I don't like it either." He shivered. "Can we go?"

That seemed to spur Ra back into action. "Of course." He held his hand out to Frey, and Frey was happy to take it.

Instead of trudging back to the cave entrance, Ra moved them there with his powers. The sun was shining now, but the air was still humid, and the feeling made Frey shiver. He wasn't cold, but he couldn't wait to go home and take a hot shower.

"Do you have any suspects?" he asked.

Ra looked down at the town. It was still half covered in water, but hopefully, without the rain coming down, it wouldn't get worse. "I haven't kept up with the minor gods, unfortunately," Ra said. "I don't want to think it could be a major one, but it's a possibility."

"You don't think so, though."

"The minor gods weren't as involved in the fight with Apophis as the major ones. They know what happened, but they haven't seen it with their own eyes, especially the younger ones. The older gods, the most powerful ones, know what Apophis is planning and what they stand to lose if he gets out of the underworld. The minor gods, especially the ones who want more power for themselves, would be easier to recruit." Ra shook his head. "But there are so many of them that I can't be sure who's responsible for this."

"You don't have to guess. We'll find out eventually."

"I'm worried about how long it'll take us."

That worried Frey, too, but they were doing the best they could.

They headed back to town and went to work helping the humans. Here, they were warier and tended to stay away, but that didn't matter. It didn't stop Ra and Frey from doing what they could, but Frey was still thinking about the conversation he and Ra had in the cave.

It was obvious and understandable that Ra didn't want to believe someone from his pantheon was doing this, even a minor god. He'd been isolated for so long, and maybe he didn't fully realize how nasty some of the gods could be. Frey wasn't surprised a god had decided they wanted more power and that they were ready to do anything to get it, including hurting humans. Most of them wouldn't have thought twice about doing something like that, which was one more reason it was hard to find out who was behind all of this.

Frey was so busy thinking about what was happening that he got distracted. He put his foot down and felt something move under it, but by the time he realized he was about to slip, it was too late. His foot slid forward while the rest of his body went backward. He reached for his power, hoping he'd have enough time to move away, but a strong arm wrapped around his waist before he could. He was pulled against a hard chest, and he looked up, relieved to find Ra looking down at him.

"Everything okay?" Ra asked.

Frey nodded and started to move away, but he slipped again. He landed against Ra's chest a second time and clutched at Ra's shoulders. Ra wrapped his arms around Frey and held him close, and when Frey looked up, he could read something other than worry in Ra's gaze.

Last time, Ra had kissed him. This time, Frey took that step, pushing up on his tiptoes so he could reach Ra's lips. He pressed them together, once, twice, Ra's warmth seeping into him as he did so. One of Ra's hands snaked upwards to cup the back of Frey's head, and Ra held him in place as he finally kissed him like he meant it.

Even though they were in the middle of a disaster, this felt like heaven. Frey never wanted it to end. Even though he was on slippery ground and the world was coming down around them, he felt safe in Ra's arms. Their problems were still waiting for them, and they'd have to go back to them eventually. For now, though, Frey was perfectly happy in Ra's arms and had no intention of stepping away.

Ever.

Ra was surprised at the strength of what he felt for Frey. He'd been trying to keep it to himself, but with Frey in his arms, it wasn't possible anymore. Clearly, Frey wanted him as much as he wanted Frey.

Ra was used to being wanted. Being who he was, he had gods throwing themselves at him almost daily when he left his wing of the palace. He suspected that humans would do the same if he visited the human world more often. He was an attractive man, but he suspected that wasn't what most people wanted from him. It was his power, what he could give them.

But none of that applied to Frey. Ra had observed him as they lived together. Frey was quiet, and he didn't want power. He was content with what he had, with helping humans have sunny days and good harvests. He enjoyed walks along the lake and playing with his boar. He wouldn't know what to do with Ra's power, and that was refreshing.

Ra wasn't sure he'd ever been wanted for anything but his

power. He *knew* he'd never been wanted for himself until today. He wasn't quite sure how to deal with that or what to do about it, so he continued kissing Frey.

He never wanted to stop.

It was foolish of him to feel so strongly for a god who belonged in a different pantheon, but he felt closer to Frey than he had felt to most of his family in years. Even now that he was closer to some of his family members, Frey was still at the center of his mind and life.

He pulled Frey even closer, needing more. Frey raised a leg, hooked it around Ra's thigh, and Ra started hauling him up.

That was when the ground shifted under him. He tilted back, his feet going the other way and slipping forward. Frey yelped and put his foot back on the ground, and they held each other in an attempt to stay on their feet.

"We probably shouldn't be doing this here," Frey murmured.

His cheeks were flushed and his lips slick. Ra wanted nothing more than to keep him in his arms, but he nodded. "We'll get hurt if we continue."

"And it's not why we're here. We should head back and help the humans."

For a moment, Ra had been able to stop thinking about the disaster happening so close to them. He'd lost himself in Frey, but neither of them could allow it to continue any longer. They were here for a reason, as Frey had mentioned.

Ra shuffled his feet away from Frey. "You're right. We should go and do what we can to help." Should Ra thank Frey for the kiss? Should he tell him how much he'd enjoyed it? It felt like he should say something, but he didn't know what.

Ra had never felt so awkward. He wasn't sure if it was because of who Frey was or how strong Ra's feelings for him were. Either way, Ra despised feeling as awkward as he did.

It was different from the way he behaved in the rest of his life, or at least, the way he'd behaved until he'd become more involved in the human world. He supposed it had been easy to be smooth and authoritative when he was on his own in his wing of the palace. The other gods had mostly left him alone, and when someone had needed to talk to him, they treated him like the powerful god he was. They'd been family, and Ra had been in a place he was familiar with.

Nothing in his life right now was familiar.

He started to move, eager to get to work, but a hand on his forearm stopped him. He turned to look at Frey.

Frey smiled softly. "I enjoyed the kiss."

Luckily, Ra didn't blush, even though his cheeks felt heated. "I enjoyed it, too."

"We should do it again soon."

Ra's heart swelled. "I agree."

That seemed to help Frey relax. "Good."

Maybe Ra wasn't the only one who felt awkward. It seemed to him that Frey wasn't sure what to say, either, and it helped soothe something in him. He wasn't as smooth and seductive as he wanted to be, but neither was Frey. That didn't mean Ra wasn't attracted to him, and he hoped the same went for Frey. Maybe they could find a way not to be awkward together.

Ra was a millennia-old god. He'd gone to battle with Apophis and had fought dozens of minor gods. A kiss shouldn't ruffle him the way this one had.

To Ra's surprise, Frey leaned closer and kissed his cheek. "Let's go, then."

When Frey offered his hand, Ra could only take it. He'd go wherever Frey took him, which wasn't a feeling he was used to. He didn't know what it was about Frey, but he didn't care. He wanted the other god in his life, and hopefully, soon in his bed. But even if that never happened, Frey was the first person in a long time Ra could remember feeling so close to, so he'd take whatever Frey was ready to offer. It didn't matter if Frey never wanted anything more than kisses. It didn't matter if he didn't want that, either. Ra would agree to anything to keep Frey in his life.

Frey moved them back to the first area where they'd appeared. Now that the rain had stopped, the humans had started working on trying to get the people stuck on their houses out of there, and small boats drifted by. It would be simple for Ra to start helping, but no matter how powerful he was, he couldn't work miracles. That hurt, because he wanted to erase all the pain Apophis was causing.

"We have to find out who's behind this," he muttered, looking around. His hands itched for him to start working.

"I agree," Frey answered. "We need to stop whoever this is from hurting more humans. They don't deserve this."

"We have to start talking to the gods on our list."

Ra wasn't looking forward to that. It wasn't just that he could think of nothing more bothersome than dealing with his extended family. It was also that, generally, he didn't like people, especially other gods. He knew the ones who belonged in his pantheon. A few were nice, like Qebui and Sed, but most were full of themselves. They wouldn't care what was happening to the human world. Hopefully, they *would* care once they found out Apophis was involved, but Ra wasn't looking forward to dealing with their reaction when they did. It was necessary, so he'd do it, but he'd rather stick around here and help the humans.

"Let's get started," he said, cracking his knuckles.

Frey's expression was grim when he nodded. He felt the same way Ra did. They knew this wasn't the worst of it, and that soon, Apophis would try again. What they were doing helped, but not nearly enough. The only thing they could do that would solve the problems the human world had to deal with at the moment was find Apophis's ally and stop both of them.

Would they be able to do that?

Chapter Eight

"Do we really have to do this?" Ra grumbled.

Frey was sitting next to him, staring at the group of people in front of them.

Ra should have known something was happening when Loki had called to ask him to meet him at the palace in Egypt. He hadn't known what to expect, but the noise and people weren't surprising.

What *was* surprising was that they all wanted to help.

"They care about you and what's happening," Frey murmured.

They'd appeared in Jimmy's office, and he'd made them sit down on one of the couches. Loki was already there, alone this time, which was odd. Ra wondered where his son was. Maybe with Sam.

Loki wasn't the only one present. Jimmy and Mery, the current pharaoh, were there, along with Qebui and Sed. Mery was quiet, but Jimmy didn't seem to know the meaning of the word.

"We want to help," he said, facing Qebui.

"I understand, and I'm all for you coming to the sky palace, but not right now. You have work to do."

Jimmy's eyes narrowed. "I don't need you to remind me that I have work to do. But this is important. I'm sure Mery can do without me for half the day."

Mery looked up, blinking. He'd been reading something on his phone, but he quickly put it away when he realized he was being pulled into the conversation. "I agree that this is important, and I want to help as much as you do, Jimmy, but Qebui is right. You and I are human, and that's who we should focus on. We have plenty of work to do here, making sure the country is safe. We haven't been hit by any of the disasters yet, but I wouldn't be surprised if Apophis targeted us soon. He's bound to realize Ra is trying to stop him, and even though I don't know him, I doubt he'll take it well."

Ra already knew Apophis wouldn't. If they managed to find Apophis's ally and get rid of them, Apophis would try to get revenge. Hopefully, taking away his ally in the human world would be enough to make him retreat. Osiris had sent word that Apophis was still stuck in the underworld. There should be no way for him to come out, and with his ally gone, no one would be raising demons.

The demons came straight from the underworld, and they gave Apophis more power. Their presence in the human world made it easier for Apophis to create the disasters. If they were gone, he wouldn't have an anchor here anymore, and he'd have to find another way to influence the human world.

Hopefully, it would take him several decades, or better, hundreds of years.

"You're afraid I'll get hurt," Jimmy accused.

Mery didn't seem to care about Jimmy's tone. "Of course I am. We all are. You and I have to face the reality that even though we're dating gods, we're only human. As much as we want to help, it's not our place. Do you think Qebui would be able to focus if he kept worrying about one of the gods attacking you? What if they find Apophis's ally? I doubt whoever it is will just stand there and let them arrest him or whatever they'll do to deal with them."

Jimmy sighed. "Fine. But we're coming up for dinner. I want to see Nu. It's been too long."

The tension in the room lifted. Ra understood why Jimmy

wanted to be involved. He'd want the same, even if he weren't a god. Luckily for him, or maybe unluckily, he was one, which meant he was involved.

Once Jimmy had relented, it didn't take everyone else long to get to the sky palace. Ra and Frey were there, along with Qebui, Sed, and Loki. Nu had mentioned they wanted to be part of this, but Ra wasn't sure it was a good idea. They were the parent of every god in the pantheon. They hadn't birthed all of them, but they all descended from them. It couldn't be easy to know that someone in your family, perhaps someone they were close to, was working with Apophis.

"Who do we start with?" Loki asked.

Ra and Frey had talked about it. They'd made a list of minor gods associated with lions or cats in general. A few names on the list scared Ra because he didn't want those gods to be involved, so the sooner he made sure they weren't, the better it would be. "How about Bastet?" he suggested.

Loki frowned. "Isn't she a cat?"

"Yes, cats are the animals she's associated with."

"Why are we looking into her, then?"

"Because we can't be sure the humans saw a lion."

Loki snorted. "I suppose. There's a big difference between a lion and a cat, though."

"Let's go talk to her," Ra said with a sigh.

They did. Luckily for them, when Bastet opened her door, she smiled. She was Ra's daughter, and his heart would break if she was involved.

"Father. It's been a long time since you visited me."

Ra found himself smiling back. "I apologize for that. I should have come sooner."

"Don't worry. I understand why you didn't." She hesitated. "I have to warn you that Sekmet is here, though."

She was another god Ra hoped wasn't involved in this. She was technically his daughter, since he'd created her from

Hathor, another of his daughters. She'd almost killed the entire human world, and it was all because of Ra. He'd stopped her by dying beer the color of blood and getting her drunk. Once she'd woken up, she'd been calmer, but she'd never stopped being fierce. As far as he knew, she'd stayed away from the humans since then. He hoped that was still true and that neither she nor Bastet had anything to do with this.

He smiled. "I need to talk to both of you, so that's actually a good thing."

Bastet seemed hesitant. "Are you sure?"

"We have to do this. I apologize."

She looked behind Ra at the other gods gathered there. "I suppose you should come in. I can see that whatever happened, it's important."

They walked in, and she guided them to a sitting area. Ra tensed when he noticed Sekmet, even though Bastet had warned him. Sekmet's eyes narrowed when she saw Ra, and her head shifted from that of a beautiful young woman with black hair and black eyes to a lion's head.

Frey sucked in a breath next to Ra, and Ra pressed a hand to the small of his back.

"I'm sorry to bother you," he said. "But it's good to see you both."

Sekmet snorted. "Sure it is. What do you want?"

"Have you heard about the natural disasters happening in the human world?"

Sekmet's eyes narrowed. It was uncanny to see a lion do that. "You think it was me?"

"No. I don't believe you and Bastet are involved. I just need to be sure. I'd also like to know if either of you knows anything about it. Maybe you've heard someone talk about it or noticed someone behaving strangely."

"I haven't," Bastet said as she sat beside her sister. She had dark hair and eyes, too, but where Sekmet was tall and strong,

Bastet was lithe and graceful.

It was good to see that they got along. Ra had five daughters and one son. Two of his daughters were associated with lions, Sekmet and Tefnut. He was planning on visiting Tefnut next, but he'd been the most worried about Sekmet, considering her past and why he'd created her.

Luckily, neither she nor Bastet had anything to do with Apophis. Sekmet got so offended that Ra had suggested it that she almost stormed out. The only reason she didn't was that Bastet stopped her. Sekmet was easy to anger and difficult to calm, so the fact that Bastet had a calming effect on her could only be a good thing, especially when she told him that the two of them spent most of their time together. They'd become friends, something Ra had missed while he'd been hiding in his wing of the palace after retiring because of what he'd done to Sekmet.

Ra was no closer to having answers to his questions when he and the others left his daughters behind. Unfortunately, they'd just started on their list.

"Who's next?" Loki asked.

"One of my other daughters, Tefnut."

"With so many children, why don't you give me tips on raising kids?"

"Your son isn't your first child. Shouldn't you know how to deal with children?"

Loki waved Ra's words away. "He's not my first child, but if you remember, one of my children is a wolf, another is a snake, and another is a horse."

Ra supposed it was different to raise a half-human child, although he didn't have any experience with that.

The day wore on. Thankfully, no one Ra was closely related to seemed to be involved. They could be lying, but Ra liked to think they weren't and that he'd be able to tell if they were. Unfortunately, it took them most of the day to talk to just a few people, and by the time evening arrived, Ra still didn't know who was involved. Since they'd agreed to meet Nu once they were done, they headed there. Ra had no doubt Nu would rope all of them into having dinner, and maybe that wasn't a bad thing.

Ra had isolated himself from the rest of his family for hundreds of years, so much so that watching Qebui and Jimmy, along with the others, had made him feel like he was on the outside looking in. They were close, but Ra wasn't part of their close group, and it was entirely his fault.

But maybe there was a way to change that. Maybe he could become as close to them as they were to each other. He suspected that the best way to obtain that was to spend more time with them, and he was strangely looking forward to dinner.

Especially since Frey would be there, too.

Frey didn't understand half of the conversations happening around him. So many names he didn't recognize were being thrown around that it made his head ache, and it was safer for him to focus on his dinner and not engage. Besides, what could he contribute? He was here to support Ra, and he would, but his pantheon wasn't the one involved. He didn't have a say in any of this.

Even with all of that, Frey felt relaxed. He didn't quite belong, but no one was planning to use him to do something he disagreed with, and no one was threatening him. It was different from Asgard, where Frey had been forced to keep to himself unless he wanted to be pulled into one of Odin's plans. Here, he could breathe and let go of the tension, especially with Ra by his side. If there was one person Frey trusted completely, it was Ra.

Things changed again when Sam arrived with two other humans and Sed. Frey knew who the humans were, but he didn't think he'd ever talked to them. He'd never been close to anyone in the Egyptian pantheon until he'd allied with them to save Loki, and while these humans weren't gods, Frey didn't know how to behave.

He decided that staying where he was and keeping his distance would be for the best, but he hadn't counted on the humans wanting to talk to him.

"So, you're Ra's boo?" Jimmy asked after introducing himself.

Frey turned wide eyes to Ra while everyone around the table focused on them. Loki cackled, and Frey had to resist the urge to glare at him. How should he answer that question? He and Ra hadn't talked about what they were. They hadn't had time, with everything happening and their hunt for Apophis's ally.

But Frey wanted to find the answer. He wanted to know what Ra saw him as and what he wished for them to be.

"Boo?" Ra delicately asked as if he couldn't quite say the word.

Jimmy grinned. "You know — boyfriend? Partner? I'd say lover, but it sounds a bit old, although I guess that both of you *are* old."

Ra glanced at Frey. Frey held his breath. Would Ra be ashamed of the few kisses they'd shared? He hadn't seemed to be, but he might not want to share with his family. Frey belonged to another pantheon, after all. Once all of this was over, it would be normal and expected for him to go back to Asgard without looking back.

He swallowed. He wouldn't be able to do that. He'd fallen in love with Ra, and he doubted he could forget him, no matter how hard he tried. Ra wasn't someone he could stop thinking about.

"Most people are old compared to you," Ra said.

Jimmy laughed. "You're not wrong. You didn't answer my

question, though."

Ra hesitated, and Frey steeled himself for the disappointment. He should have expected it. They hadn't talked about this or what would happen once Apophis was dealt with. They couldn't even be sure they'd win that battle.

"I wouldn't call him my *boo*, but Frey is special to me," Ra finally said.

Jimmy wiggled his eyebrows. "Special, how?"

Frey pressed his lips together. Why was Jimmy pushing so hard? Frey wanted to know, too, but he didn't want Ra to feel like he had to answer.

Ra looked down at Frey. He was smiling, and Frey's heart skipped a beat. No one should be so handsome, not even a god.

"Special in the way Qebui is special to you," Ra murmured.

Frey couldn't hear anyone else around the table. He could only see Ra and hear his words as he told everyone that he loved Frey.

"I didn't know," he whispered.

Ra's smile didn't waver. "I should have told you sooner."

"Maybe, but I should have told you that I feel the same."

"The important thing is that we know now."

Frey's heart felt lighter, and he couldn't snuff out the smile that spread his lips. "It is." Whatever happened next with Apophis, this was something Frey would fight to keep.

Ra was worth fighting for, as was his family.

Things were even more relaxed after the short conversation with Jimmy. It seemed to have been enough for everyone around the table to accept Frey as family, which was bewildering, but Frey liked it. He'd longed to have something like this, but he'd never found it with his own family in Asgard.

He had now.

They'd all have to fight a war before they could live in peace, but having this was worth it. Frey would defend anyone around this table to the death, but especially the god sitting next to him. Ra was his, and he wouldn't allow anyone to touch the god, not even Apophis.

Once dinner was over, people started drifting away. Frey was full of food and love, and he couldn't wait to be alone with Ra. Would they go home to their little house in Finland?

"You two should stay here," Nu said after saying goodbye to Sam and Loki.

"We should go home," Ra answered. He hooked an arm around Frey's waist in an uncharacteristic show of affection.

Ra was always a little tense and clumsy when it came to feelings and physical signs of affection. It meant a lot that he was doing this, and Frey leaned against him.

Nu smiled. "As you wish. Just remember that this will always be your home. Whenever you need us, for whatever you need us, we'll be here. All of us. You're not alone, Ra. You never were, not even back when the situation with Sekmet arose. It's good to have you back, even though it's for a dreadful reason. Don't stay away for so long again, please."

Ra lightly bowed his head and leaned forward to kiss his parent's cheek. "I won't. It's time for Frey and me to go home, but we'll be back."

They would. They had to find Apophis's ally, and they lived between these walls. But Frey suspected that wouldn't be the only reason Ra would come. Like Frey, he'd realized he had a family, and he wouldn't abandon them.

It took another fifteen minutes to extricate themselves from Nu and the others who still lingered there, but it felt good. It felt better to be home, though, and once they were, Frey closed his eyes and took a deep breath. He'd loved dinner, but was glad to be alone with Ra.

But what would they do now? Ra had admitted to his family that he cared for Frey and viewed him as a lover, even though they hadn't gotten that far — yet.

Frey cleared his throat as Ra turned toward him.

"I hope you're not angry over what I told Jimmy at dinner," Ra said stiffly.

"I'm not." If anything, Frey was relieved. He could see he'd have to be the one to take the next step, though. Ra clearly didn't know how to behave. Frey wasn't sure, either, but he knew what he wanted. "I'm glad you told them that. I want to be important to you."

"You are."

Frey turned to face Ra fully. "I want more than kisses."

Ra swallowed. His Adam's apple bobbed, capturing Frey's attention. He leaned forward and rose on his tiptoes, pressing a kiss there.

Ra sucked in a breath. He didn't push Frey away, which Frey hoped was a good sign. He kissed upward, following the shape of Ra's jaw until he reached Ra's lips. They parted to welcome him as Ra's arms wrapped around him and pulled him close.

The kiss was slow and made Frey burn brighter. He wanted more, and he gently pushed Ra toward the hallway that led to their bedrooms. Ra blinked at him as if he were awakening from a dream, and Frey waited.

"What do you want?" Ra asked.

"You."

"You have me."

"Yeah?"

Ra appeared solemn as he nodded. "For now and forever, if you'll have me."

Frey beamed. "I do."

Ra let Frey pull him to his bedroom. He wanted what was about to happen as much as Frey, but he was hesitant. Would he be able to give Frey what he desired? It had been so long since he'd last had a lover that he wasn't sure. He remembered the physical aspect, of course, but he'd never felt for any of his lovers the way he felt for Frey. He'd never wanted anything more than sex and wasn't sure how to behave.

"Don't fret," Frey said as they walked into his bedroom. "Whatever you're ready for, we'll do."

"I just don't want to hurt or disappoint you."

Frey's smile was blinding even in the darkness. "Nothing you can do would disappoint me. Why don't you take a moment in the bathroom to think? Wash up and get ready for the night?"

That wasn't what Ra had expected. "What will you do?"

"The same. I'll wait for you here."

Ra wanted a moment to think, so after kissing Frey, he headed to his bedroom. A tiny bathroom was attached, and he took his time to strip and wash his hands and face. He also brushed his teeth. All of that took him only a few minutes, and when he was done, he hovered by the bedroom door, wondering what was next.

He'd put on the pants he slept in and nothing else. It felt good not to be restrained by clothing, but now that he was ready, he was still hesitant. He and Frey wanted the same thing. They could have it. Why did he feel like making a mistake would destroy everything?

But he wasn't making a mistake, and he wouldn't. Frey was strong and wouldn't hesitate to tell Ra if Ra did something he didn't want or wasn't ready for. They both would.

There was nothing for Ra to worry about. He trusted Frey, which meant he could relax and let this happen. He'd wanted it for weeks, and it was finally in reach.

Ra nodded and stepped into the hallway. He walked down to Frey's bedroom, anticipating what would come next.

He froze as he stepped into the bedroom. Frey was naked on top of the covers, a bottle of something by his side. His legs were spread, and one of his hands was between his legs. He looked up but didn't try to hide from Ra's gaze.

He was beautiful.

Ra couldn't move. He couldn't do anything but watch as Frey's hand moved. It was too easy to imagine what he was doing and where his fingers were. Ra had believed he'd be the one to do that, and he wanted to, but he was enthralled.

Frey looked at Ra, his hand still moving. "Are you going to stand there and watch me fuck myself on my fingers?"

Ra swallowed at the words. Was he?

No.

He got naked in seconds, pushing his pants down and leaving them on the floor where they fell. He had a perfect view of what was happening between Frey's legs when he knelt on the edge of the mattress, but it wasn't enough anymore, especially when Frey used the bottle to slick his fingers again, then pushed three of them into his body.

Ra moved forward until he was between Frey's legs. Frey continued moving while reaching for the bottle next to him. "Use that," he ordered. He sounded breathless.

Ra took the bottle and looked down at it. It had to be some kind of lubricant, which he and Frey would need. He tried to open it, but it felt slick, and he fumbled with it, almost dropping it. He swallowed and picked it back up. When he finally managed to open it, he breathed easier, but they were just starting.

He slicked his fingers, relieved to be able to let go of the bottle again. His hand trembled as he touched his cock. He told himself that he was a powerful god and that he'd done this before, but these feelings were so strong that they were taking over. He was so nervous that he didn't know what to do or how to make this good for Frey.

Frey removed his fingers from his body and raised his knees to his chest, making his intentions clear. Ra couldn't look away, and he didn't want to. But the voice in the back of his head was strong, and it was telling him that he had to convince Frey that he could give him anything he wanted so Frey would never even think of leaving.

Frey let his legs fall and sat up, startling Ra. "I'm pushing too hard," Frey said.

Ra didn't know how to answer that. He didn't want to stop, but he *was* overwhelmed. That wasn't like him, which made him feel even more unbalanced. "I'm fine."

"You need to be more convincing if you want me to believe that." Frey opened his arms. "Come here. We don't have to rush into anything. I apologize if I was too forward."

Ra didn't hesitate. He leaned down and pressed his body against Frey's. It felt like coming home — like he'd always belonged here and like he always would. Frey shivered and wrapped his arms around him, holding him close as he stroked his back.

Ra allowed his feelings to settle. This was what he wanted, and so did Frey. It didn't matter if it wasn't perfect or if either of them made mistakes. Frey wouldn't care, just like Ra didn't. He didn't have a reason to be so nervous, even with his feelings. He wasn't the only one to have them. Frey was right there with him, and this was as important to him as it was to Ra.

Ra pressed closer. His cock slipped between Frey's ass cheeks, and he froze. They'd stopped this. What would Frey think of Ra's erect cock poking at him?

But Frey just kissed Ra's cheek and reached between them. Ra reminded himself that none of this mattered. Only their feelings did, and the sex was an extension of them. It was a way to show each other how they felt, and feelings were strong and messy. The only important thing was that they were there.

Frey moved slowly as he hooked his legs around Ra's waist

and reached between them, as if he expected Ra to push him away. Ra couldn't have even if he'd wanted to, and he didn't. Through this, he could show Frey how he felt about him even when he didn't have the words. Frey's fingers closed around Ra's cock. He stroked it a few times before pressing the head between his legs, but he didn't move. He looked up at Ra, and Ra knew he'd have to be the one to take the next step.

He pressed a kiss to Frey's lips, then to his jaw, neck, and lower, to his collarbone. It pushed his hips away from Frey's body, but not for long. He moved forward again, letting Frey angle him the way he needed, and pushed.

His cock slipped into Frey. It was tight and overwhelming, pulling Ra deeper inside. Frey let go and grabbed Ra's shoulders, pulling him down to kiss him. His body opened to Ra, welcoming him home, and Ra pushed until his hips met Frey's groin. He couldn't go any further. He and Frey were one.

Ra couldn't name the emotions threatening to spill out of his lips. They were too strong, and he didn't want to overwhelm Frey. He felt enough of that himself and thought his actions spoke loud enough that Frey would understand.

There was none of the awkwardness Ra had felt when he'd had sex in the past. He'd stay with Frey even when this was over, and it would never be truly over. After tonight, they'd do this again and again, every time they wanted to. They'd kiss as often as they could. They'd have forever to be together, which was both intimidating and incredible.

Frey tilted his hips and pushed up as Ra thrust forward. It was easy to follow his instincts, to continue to move and make Frey his in every way possible. He wanted to bring Frey as much pleasure as possible, so Ra pressed his body harder against Frey's. Frey cried out and dug his fingers into Ra's shoulders, pushing his cock against him. He shuddered as Ra angled his hips, thrusting deeper than he had before. He could feel Frey's cock rub against his stomach, the head damp and leaving a trail on Ra's skin as if marking him.

Frey tightened around Ra's cock and his entire body tensed. He threw his head back, shuddering one last time before he came, slicking both their stomachs with his release. His body pulled Ra in as it pulsed around him, and Ra stopped resisting. This was perfect. He didn't need to do more or differently.

He pushed forward one last time, filling Frey's body and holding him as he gave in to the pleasure. He could feel Frey's hands on his skin, skimming his shoulders and stroking down his back, murmuring words Ra didn't understand in a language that sounded native on Frey's lips.

Ra loved him. He'd never felt this way for anyone else, and it had taken him a while to understand what he felt, but he knew now. He wanted to be with Frey forever if Frey would have him.

It was terrifying. Ra was powerful, but Frey could kill him with barely a word. Ra had never been so vulnerable.

But he trusted Frey with his life and, more importantly, with his heart.

CHAPTER NINE

"How dare you suggest I'm involved?" Mehyt asked, straightening her back and glaring at Ra.

Ra raised his hands to fend off her anger. "I don't believe you are."

Her glare didn't lessen. "You wouldn't be here talking to me if you didn't believe I was helping Apophis. How can you think that after everything he's done?"

"We've been talking to everyone associated with lions. We even talked to Bastet, and her animal is a cat. This has nothing to do with you. We're just trying to find out who's helping Apophis, and since a lion was seen, that's the way we went. If people had seen a buffalo, we'd be talking to every god associated with those."

Mehyt didn't seem relieved by that. If anything, she appeared even angrier. "Well, I have nothing to do with Apophis and never will. You should leave."

Ra was impressed. Few gods would dare talk to him that way, and all of them were almost as powerful as he was. Mehyt was a minor goddess from the early dynastic period. She was associated with a lioness, which was why Ra and the others were talking to her.

This time around, it was just him, Frey, and Qebui. Loki had stayed behind with his son while Sed was with his pharaoh. Ra didn't blame either one of them. He'd rather be anywhere but here, too.

No matter how minor Mehyt was, Ra didn't want to antagonize her, so he inclined his head to her and got to his feet.

"Once again, I'm sorry about all of this. We're just trying to keep everyone safe."

"And you're doing so by insulting people and insinuating they're involved?"

Qebui cleared his throat. He was a minor god, too, and while he and Ra were much more familiar with each other than Ra was with Mehyt, Qebui would never have dared talk to Ra this way.

Thankfully, they didn't have to linger. Once they were back in the hallway, Ra sighed. "I don't think it was her."

"I don't know. She seemed quite angry at you," Qebui pointed out.

"Probably because I insulted her by insinuating she's associated with Apophis. No one wants that, and I expect Apophis's ally to react the same way."

"Maybe so, but she has a place in our pantheon, and it's not acceptable for her to talk to you that way."

Ra was surprised at how fiercely Qebui defended him. "It doesn't matter how powerful I am. I'm still just a god."

"You're not just a god. You're the sun god, and it means a lot for our pantheon and our people. You shouldn't allow people to talk to you that way. You need to show them you're still in control and as powerful as you were before." Qebui hesitated. "I'm afraid some of them might not want to help us otherwise. They won't want to be involved if they think you'll lose to Apophis."

Ra rubbed his forehead. "You're right. If someone else talks to me that way, I'll put them back in their place. Who's next on our list?"

Frey took out his phone. "Someone named Ipy."

Ra nodded. "A minor goddess of fertility."

"She's associated with lions?"

"Yes, along with crocodiles and hippopotamuses. I doubt she has much to do with this."

"That's what you say every time, but one of them *is* involved. We know that for sure."

"We do, but she can't turn into a feline. I put her on the list because I wanted to be thorough, that's all." And knowing she wasn't involved made Ra feel better. He wasn't going into this conversation dreading what would happen like he had for previous ones.

Still, they needed to find something, and so far, no one they'd talked to had been involved. Either Apophis's ally was incredibly good at lying, or they hadn't talked to them yet.

"Maybe you should bring in Maat," Qebui suggested.

Ra shook his head as soon as he heard the name. "She has more important things to do."

"Does she? Because to me, it feels like the most important thing right now is stopping Apophis."

Maat was another one of Ra's daughters. She represented truth, balance, and justice, and she'd know if someone was lying. But Ra didn't want to pull her in. He felt he already had enough people looking for Apophis's ally. He'd need all the help he could find if he ever had to face Apophis, but hopefully, it wouldn't come to that.

Since they were already in the wing where the minor gods lived, it was easy to find Ipy's door. She opened quickly, and they were faced with a woman with a hippopotamus head.

"Yes?" she asked, bowing to Ra.

"I apologize for bothering you, but we'd like to ask you a few questions."

She stepped aside to let them in. Her rooms were much smaller than Ra's, but she was a minor goddess. Like all the rooms in the palace, though, they opened into the garden. There was a wide lake, and Ra had no doubt she took advantage of it as much as she could. She probably swam there every day.

"I already know what you're going to ask," she said.

"People have been talking."

Ra had known they would. People always talked, especially gods. They were a bunch of gossipy people who didn't have anything better to do.

"So you know we want to ask you about Apophis."

"Would you believe me if I told you I had nothing to do with him?"

"We believed everyone else, so I don't see why we shouldn't believe you."

She nodded. "Well, I do not have anything to do with him. I've never seen him. I was never strong enough to go against him, so I wasn't part of the fight." She hesitated, then squared her shoulders and looked straight at Ra. "But this time, I want to help. I don't know if I'll be able to do much, but I'll be there."

Ra exchanged a glance with Frey and Qebui. He doubted either god believed she was involved, and he didn't have a problem with her helping. Even if she didn't manage much, they could use everyone they could gather.

Frey's phone made a sound, and he retrieved it from his pocket with a frown. His eyes widened as he read something on the screen, and Ra steeled himself for the next bad news. Apophis had struck again. Ra didn't have to ask to know that was the problem, and once again, he berated himself for not being fast enough. When would all of this stop?

"A tsunami," Frey said. "Part of the town is gone. The rest is underwater."

Ra nodded curtly. "Do you know if anyone is headed there?"

"I got a text from Loki."

"I'll go, too," Ipy said. "I deal well with water. I'll be able to help the humans."

"Are you sure?"

She nodded again, and her head became human. "I don't

want to scare them, so I'll go like this. It won't stop me from being able to swim."

"Thank you. We'll come, too." There was nowhere else Ra could go and nowhere else he *wanted* to go.

Humans were paying for Apophis's anger and his need for revenge. Apophis was angry at Ra, not at the humans, but to him, they were negligible. They didn't matter beyond the fact that hurting them hurt Ra. He wouldn't hesitate to continue doing this until Ra finally stopped him.

But Ra didn't know how to do that.

He needed to talk to Osiris again, but first, he had to focus on this. As long as Osiris confirmed that Apophis was still in the underworld, things weren't desperate. They would be if Apophis managed to escape, but for now, he was getting his revenge by hurting humans. Once he was out, he'd go directly to Ra, and Ra would be ready for him.

Or at least, he hoped so.

All of this was horrifying, and once again, Frey wasn't doing enough to help.

They were doing everything they could to stop Apophis, but it still wasn't enough. They needed more—more time, more gods who could help the humans deal with the aftermath of these disasters, more help finding Apophis's ally.

Frey swallowed. He hadn't wanted to do this, but maybe it was time to go to his own pantheon. He wasn't sure anyone would help, but it was worth asking.

He looked around, trying to find Ra. He noticed him as he was coming out of a house, carrying an elderly man. Frey made a beeline for them, helping the man to his feet before turning to Ra as the man was taken away by other humans. "I have to go to Asgard."

Ra frowned. "Why would you?"

"Because we need more help. It's good to have Loki and the others, but we need more gods."

"And you believe you'll be able to convince your family to help?"

"I don't know, but I have to try." Gods were powerful and thought nothing of playing with humans. Surely, they'd step in now that those humans needed their help?

"I'll come with you."

"I don't think that's the best idea. If Odin sees you there, it won't end well, and we can't make another powerful enemy. We have enough on our hands with Apophis."

"I have half a mind of going down to the underworld and getting rid of him permanently," Ra grumbled.

But Frey knew that Ra would have already done it if it was that easy. Apophis was powerful, possibly even more powerful than Ra. Ra had needed help from his pantheon when he'd locked Apophis away in the underworld, and he'd need them this time, too.

"Just let me try. I promise I'll be careful."

"I don't doubt that. I'm just not comfortable knowing you're there, especially after what you told me about the other Norse gods."

"I'll go with him," Loki declared as he strode toward them.

Frey didn't ask how he'd heard the conversation. The how didn't matter, anyway. "You can't. Things didn't end well between you, Odin, and Thor."

"Do I look like I care? Because I don't. I'm a Norse god, which means Asgard is my home as much as it is theirs. Besides, they're not the first gods who tried killing me. I'll be fine." He patted Frey's shoulder. "I'll have you, won't I?"

"You know as well as I do that I won't be able to stand up to Odin or Thor."

"Maybe, maybe not. I doubt we'll be alone, though."

"Won't we? I'm not stupid. I realize this is a long shot."

Loki nodded. "But you have to try. We both do."

Frey wasn't looking forward to it, but he was in less danger than Loki. He was tempted to ask Loki to stay back again, but he doubted anything he could say would change Loki's mind. He'd always been stubborn and seemingly unafraid of Odin's reaction to his presence in Asgard.

Frey turned to Ra. "We'll be back as soon as possible."

"We'll stay here for as long as we can." Ra looked around and grimaced. "Unfortunately, there's not much we can do."

"It's already a lot."

After the news had gone around that several gods were coming down and helping humans impacted by the disasters, most of the humans had relaxed. Frey and the others didn't have to convince them they were trying to help anymore. Every time something happened, they were welcomed, and after they'd done everything they could and were exhausted, they were usually given food and a place to rest. No matter how many times he tried to refuse the food, no one listened to him. Loki had pointed out it was rude not to take what they were sacrificing, and Frey had relented, but he didn't like it. Hopefully, soon, there would be no more disasters.

But to ensure that, they had to stop Apophis's ally.

He moved closer to Ra and quickly kissed him. "Don't get into any trouble while I'm not here," he whispered.

Ra's expression showed how worried he was. "The same goes for you. I'll storm Asgard if I have to."

"I don't think it'll come to that, but it's good to know you have my back."

"Always."

And Frey believed him.

He tore himself away from Ra, knowing he'd never leave if he didn't do so. He and Loki exchanged a glance. Then they headed to Asgard.

Frey decided to appear in front of his home. He hadn't told

Loki to do so, so he was relieved to see that Loki was already there when he arrived.

"Who do you think we can get on board?" Loki asked as he followed Frey away from the house.

"My sister." Frey was sure she'd help. "Maybe some of the minor gods. We have to try."

"I agree. We should stay away from Odin, though."

"We will. We're going to talk to Freya, anyway."

Just like Frey had expected, his sister agreed immediately. He didn't even have to explain what was happening. As soon as he said he needed her help, she said yes.

Only then did she lean forward on her couch. "Why do you need my help?"

"To make a long story short, an ancient deity from the Egyptian pantheon is trying to escape from the underworld. He's causing the disasters in the human world, and while Loki and I, along with all the gods from the Egyptian pantheon, have been trying to help, we're torn between helping the humans who need us and finding Apophis's allies in the human world. Humans are hurting, *dying*, and we can't do enough to help them."

"So you want me to go to the human world and do so myself?"

"If it's at all possible."

"I'd do anything for you, Frey."

Frey was relieved. "Do you know of anyone else who would want to help?"

She hesitated, then nodded. "I do. Come with me." She held out her hand, and Frey took it. They both looked at Loki, who rolled his eyes and grabbed Frey's shoulder.

"I'm coming just because Frey is," he said.

No matter how hard he tried to hide it, Loki was obviously nervous. It made sense after what Thor had done to him. Loki wasn't alone, but Frey wouldn't be able to do much to stop

Thor if he tried getting to Loki again.

Frey might not be of help, but Ra would move the earth and the sky to find Loki. He'd even go against Odin, and while Frey wasn't sure who would win, he'd bet his money on Ra.

They appeared in front of the house, and Freya let go of Frey's hand to knock on the door. Frey held his breath, trying to remember who lived here. The house was big, so it wasn't a minor god, but it also wasn't one of the bigger ones.

The door swung open. Loki sucked in a breath, and while it took a moment for Frey to understand who the man standing in front of them was, he understood why soon enough.

"Forseti," Freya said. "Can we come in?"

Forseti looked from Frey to Loki, then nodded. "It's probably better if you do. We wouldn't want my grandfather to find out you're here."

Because Forseti was the only son of Nanna and Baldur—Odin's now-deceased son.

"I thought we'd stay away from Odin," Loki whispered as they followed Forseti inside.

"My sister decided to come."

"Why would she think this was a good idea?"

"You'd have to ask her."

Forseti was the god of justice and reconciliation. Coming from Odin's line, he was powerful, and thankfully, he didn't seem to have as much hatred in his heart as his grandfather. Frey was still wary, but Forseti didn't do anything to try to hurt him and Loki.

They went through the same explanation they had with Freya. Frey had no idea what to expect, but he was surprised when Forseti nodded. "I'll help you."

"Your grandfather won't be happy."

"I don't care what he thinks. He's not me, and I'm not him. After what happened with my father, I don't care what he thinks or expects me to do."

That was understandable. "We should head back to the human world. They need all our help, and they need it now." Frey wanted to talk to more people, but maybe he should stop with two for today. His luck had held until now, and he doubted it would for much longer.

He realized he'd been right when the front door slammed open. Everyone shot to their feet, and Frey held his breath as Odin appeared.

Odin's gaze jumped from one god to the other. "So Thor was right. He did see you," he spat out, staring at Loki.

Loki grinned at him. "Well, Asgard is my home."

"You're not welcome in Asgard anymore. You never were. Go back to your humans and leave my grandson alone."

Forseti frowned. "I'm going back with him."

"You'll do no such thing. We don't involve ourselves in human trouble."

"Why not? Why shouldn't we, when so many of those troubles are caused by gods?"

"Because they don't matter. You're staying here, along with Frey and Freya. Loki, if you don't leave now, *I'll* make you leave."

"Oh, will you fight me?" Loki sounded strangely eager at the thought.

"I will if I have to."

Frey had enough of this. "You're an asshole," he snapped. He regretted those words as soon as they left his mouth, but not enough to take them back. "A controlling, stubborn, cruel asshole."

"How dare you?" Odin asked.

"How dare you decide what I'll do? I'm not staying here one second longer. I have a life in the human world, and I'm going back to it."

"I'll force you to stay."

"You and what army? I might be a minor god, but I'm a fighter, and you know that." As long as whatever god who wanted to fight him didn't use their power, Frey would probably win. He was a good swordsman, and he'd made sure to keep up with every kind of combat he could find.

"And he won't fight you alone," Loki said, stepping closer. "Gods don't need to be confined to Asgard. Both Frey and I have found a life with the humans, and we'll do everything we can to protect that life. If Frey's sister and your grandson want to help, they're welcome to. The only person you can force to do anything is yourself, Odin, and if I were you, I'd force myself to look in the mirror. I doubt you'll like what you see there."

With that, Loki grabbed Frey. Frey knew what was about to happen, so he took his sister's hand. He wasn't surprised to see her reach for Forseti with the other, and as a group, they disappeared.

The last thing Frey saw was Odin's face turning almost purple, and he briefly wondered if it was about to explode.

CHAPTER TEN

They were nowhere near close to having talked to every god they suspected might be Apophis's ally, but something needed to be done. Talking to gods one by one wasn't working, so Ra had come up with another plan. He'd made sure every single god in the pantheon got the message that he'd organized a meeting to talk about Apophis and what should be done against him. It would help him find out who was willing to fight against Apophis alongside him and who might be involved with Apophis himself.

Not that Ra expected every single god who'd help him to come. He knew for sure that Set wouldn't be caught dead at this meeting. He had the god's promise he'd help, and Ra believed him. It was everyone else he had problems believing.

"You look nervous," Frey said, leaning against him.

Ra looked around the room. He'd chosen his own receiving room in the sky palace, and he suspected that some of the gods were here because they were curious. Most of them had never seen his private wing.

Ra had chosen a room that was at the beginning of the wing. He didn't want these people in his private space. They might technically be his family, but he was so far removed from most of them that they were strangers, and having strangers in the place where he lived was worse.

Even though he hadn't lived here in weeks and wasn't planning on moving back.

The small house he shared with Frey in Finland was more his home than this place ever had been. They shared Frey's bedroom now, and if they didn't have to deal with Apophis and his ally, Ra would feel his life was perfect. He'd found a place to call home and that *felt* like home, and someone to share his long life with. What more could he want?

"Not nervous," he murmured.

"Anxious, then."

Ra sighed. "I'm afraid of what we're about to find out and that we won't have enough allies to face Apophis."

"You might not have to face him. If we manage to find his ally and stop them, Apophis will stay in the underworld, right?"

Ra wanted to believe that, but how could he? Apophis had been planning revenge and his escape for thousands of years. He'd found someone to help him, but even without that person, he no doubt had backup plans. Whatever those entailed might not happen now, or even next year or in the next decade, but eventually, Ra *would* have to fight Apophis and lock him up in the underworld again or kill him. Whether he did it on his own or with his pantheon behind him was still to be seen.

"For now," Ra said.

Frey nodded. "And if he does get out, you won't face him alone. I'm not going anywhere."

Ra already knew that, but it felt good to hear it.

By the time the meeting was supposed to start, there were about a dozen gods in the room. Ra hoped that others would come eventually, once they realized Apophis was a danger again, but for now, he'd deal with the ones in front of him. Luckily for him, not all of them were minor gods. He needed all the help he could find, but the most powerful the gods were, the better it would be.

"Thank you for coming," he announced.

His close family was behind him, silently supporting him. Sed and Qebui had come up from the human world, and Nu had left their wing to be there. Loki and Frey were present, too. Ra had been surprised by Loki's presence, but he'd started to realize that Loki was part of his family now, too. It didn't matter that they belonged to a different pantheon. They cared for each other, and both Loki and Frey would be there to help.

The door opened, and a minor god came in. Ra squinted, trying to remember who he was. The god was tall and thin, with long black hair with a hint of red to it. His nails were long and painted black, and he wore all-black clothing. He reminded Ra of Loki, but there was a tension in him that Loki didn't have.

"I apologize for my lateness," he said, nodding at Ra.

"That's all right."

"That's Maahes," Nu suddenly said from behind Ra, making him jump.

He glared at his parent. "Thank you for letting me know."

Nu was frowning. "There's something about him."

"What do you mean?" Ra felt it, too, but he didn't have an explanation.

"I'm not sure. I feel like I know something important about him, but I can't remember what it is."

"You will eventually."

Ra turned his attention back to the gods surrounding him. "As you know, I've called you here to talk about Apophis."

"Is he really coming back?" Mut asked. She was close to Nu, so it wasn't surprising to see her here.

"He's trying," Ra confirmed. "He's the cause of the extreme weather and disasters that have been happening in the human world. I'm sure some of you are aware of it."

"How can he do that from the underworld? Or has he already made his way to the human world?"

"He hasn't. Osiris confirmed he's still firmly stuck there, and I trust him. We believe he found an ally. He has someone here who summons demons and does his bidding. The demons make Apophis's power stronger in the human world, which is why he's been able to influence the weather so badly."

"What can we do to stop Apophis?" Maahes asked. "The only god strong enough to do that is you."

"That might well be, but all of you can help find his ally. If we stop that person, there won't be anyone left to summon demons in the human world, and Apophis's power there will lessen. I have no doubt he'll continue trying to find a way out of the underworld, but the humans will be safe."

Maahes shook his head. "They're not who I'm worried about. What will happen to *us* if we go against Apophis?"

Ra moved closer to him. He understood why minor gods were afraid of Apophis. He'd gone against Apophis once, and he was one of the most powerful gods of their pantheon, but even he was scared.

"We can't let this stop us," he explained. "Someone must stand up to Apophis, and that will be us. We might have to sacrifice things, including our lives, but what will happen if we let Apophis come back? He'll kill us anyway, and even if he doesn't, life as we know it will change. As things are, we don't have a way out of this. Either we fight and hope to win, or we let Apophis do what he wants and lose everything."

He stopped next to Maahes and put a hand on his shoulder. "You might lose your life in the fight against Apophis, but if you don't, it means that once this is over, you can come back to what you have now. Isn't that worth fighting for?" Ra had no idea what Maahes's life was like, but surely, he had something or someone to fight for.

Maahes didn't look convinced. He leaned away from Ra, dislodging his hand from his shoulder. The movement raised Maahes's scent, which made Ra wrinkle his nose. Why did Maahes smell of sulfur?

"I do have something worth fighting for," Maahes said, even tenser than before. He got to his feet. "But I'm not sure there's anything I can do to help you."

"Where are you going?"

"I'm a minor god. I'm not strong enough to fight Apophis."

"That's not true. Everyone can help, including you. Unless you'd rather not?"

Maahes's eyes narrowed. "What are you saying?"

Ra wasn't sure what he was saying, but he could tell something was happening. "What do you have that's worth fighting for? Is it a person?"

"It's none of your business. I have to go."

Ra placed himself in front of Maahes. "You're not going anywhere until you answer my questions. What are you doing here?"

"You asked everyone to come for this meeting."

That much was true. Ra might not understand technology, but it was handy when he needed to talk to his entire pantheon at once. He suspected that at least some of the older gods weren't here because they didn't know how to read emails, and he'd have to visit them one by one. He'd be happy to do so as soon as he found out what Maahes was planning.

It couldn't be this easy, could it? Ra had been looking for Apophis's ally for weeks without finding anything. Could Maahes have delivered himself into Ra's hands when he could have easily escaped by ignoring Ra's summon and not showing up?

Frey had stayed where he was, not wanting to hover over Ra as he tried to convince his people to help, but he could tell something was wrong. He was pretty sure he wasn't the only one, because Qebui, Loki, and Sed had gotten to their feet and crowded behind him. They were ready to act if they needed to, and Frey was starting to suspect they might have to.

"What's happening?" he asked Loki. Loki was more familiar with the Egyptian pantheon, so he might be able to answer the question.

"I have no idea, but it looks like this Maahes guy is hiding something. Why is he here if he's so eager to leave already?"

"Maybe he wanted to find out what the meeting was about."

"Maybe."

Frey had no idea what was happening, but he trusted Ra. Even if Maahes attacked, Ra was powerful enough to protect himself and everyone else in this room.

"Why are you really here?" Ra asked. "You have no intention of helping us fight Apophis, so what's your reason?"

Maahes stared at him for a moment before laughing. There was nothing nice about the sound. It was cold, almost cruel. "You're not as stupid as Apophis thinks you are," he eventually said. "He didn't believe you'd understand why I was here. I told him that sending me to this meeting was stupid, but he insisted. He wants to know what you're planning, and he thought this would be the easiest way to find out."

Almost as one, the gods scattered around the room took a step back. It left Maahes and Ra alone in the middle of the room, facing each other.

"You're his ally," Ra said. There was a bit of a growl to his voice.

Could they really have finally found Apophis's ally? They'd known that talking to the minor gods one by one wouldn't guarantee they'd find that person. There were too many of them, even if they only focused on the ones associated with lions. Was Maahes associated with lions?

"Dammit," Nu muttered as if they'd read Frey's mind. "He's a lion."

Frey sucked in a breath. If Maahes truly was Apophis's

ally, he shouldn't have come here. Frey understood that Apophis wanted to find out what Ra was planning, but there had to be smarter ways to do that. Not that he was going to complain. Having Maahes here meant they could stop him before things got worse in the human world.

Maahes stood up straighter. He looked around, contempt clear in his expression. "We'll win," he declared.

"Apophis didn't win the last time I had to deal with him," Ra pointed out. He sounded calm, but Frey could see that was nothing further from the truth. He'd found what he was looking for, though, and he was ready to take care of Maahes once and for all.

"He didn't have me then," Maahes snarled. "Together, we'll rise and take over this pantheon and the entire world."

Loki snorted behind Frey, getting Maahes's attention.

The lion glared. "You shouldn't be here," he snapped.

Loki didn't seem to care. "Yes, I should, and you won't just have Ra to face when the time comes. He won last time and didn't have us backing him. He does now. How do you think this is going to end for you and Apophis?"

"We're stronger than you. It doesn't matter what pantheon you belong to — Apophis will kill all of you."

"If you truly believe that, you're an idiot. Can't you see that Apophis is using you? I mean, I'm sure he enjoys having someone in the human world do his bidding, but do you think he's going to step in to save you? You won't make it out of this room alive."

Maahes took a step back as if he finally realized the kind of trouble it was in. "You can't touch me. You don't belong in my pantheon and have no right."

"He might not, but I do," Ra said. "You were foolish to believe Apophis. Whatever he told you he'd give you for this, you should have known better. Apophis doesn't share his power with anyone. He doesn't have true allies. He has servants, and once he's done using you, he'll dispatch you without a thought. You still have time to come back to us. Tell us what Apophis is planning. Help us stop him."

Frey could see Maahes wouldn't say yes to Ra's offer. His hands were shifting to paws, and he was getting ready for battle.

Frey stepped back. This wasn't his fight. He might be allied with Ra and the other Egyptian gods, but he couldn't be a part of this. Besides, he doubted Ra needed his help. He'd faced Apophis, albeit not on his own. He shouldn't have problems dealing with Maahes.

Maahes rushed Ra, but Ra had expected it. A sword appeared in his hand, and he raised it, ready for the lion god. Maahes had only shifted part of his body—his head was that of a lion now, and his hands had turned to paws tipped with claws—but it wouldn't be enough to do real damage. Luckily, Ra knew what he was doing. He sidestepped Maahes when he threw himself at him again, then stood strong as Maahes turned to face him.

"Apophis will ruin both this place and the human world," Maahes gloated. "Together, we'll rule, and you'll die. The human world will disappear in a flurry of chaos and revenge, and nothing you can do will stop that."

Ra moved so quickly that Frey barely saw him. One second, he was staring at Maahes, and the next, he was swinging his sword, suddenly right in front of the other god. Maahes stumbled back, but not before Ra's sword hit him.

Maahes reacted instinctively, throwing his hands toward the sword to protect his face. He screamed when the blade severed one of his hands from his arm. The sword glowed from the inside, telling Frey it wasn't just a weapon— Maahes's wound wasn't bleeding. The smell of burning flesh grew heavy in the room, which could only mean that the sword had sealed Maahes's injury as it cut through his wrist.

"You'll regret this," Maahes said with a growl.

He clutched his arm to his chest, looked around, and Frey knew he was about to run. He threw himself forward, or at least, he tried to. A strong arm wrapped around his waist and pulled him back, and by the time he turned around to snap at Loki to let him go, Maahes was gone.

Several of the gods in the room disappeared after him, but Ra stayed where he was. Frey slapped Loki's hands away, and when Loki let him go, he rushed to Ra.

"Are you hurt?" he asked when he reached the other god.

Ra's sword disappeared. Maahes's hand was still on the floor, and Frey was doing his best not to stare at it. He'd never had the stomach other gods had for violence, and he'd rather not have been here when all of this had happened. He'd have to get used to all of this soon. He was deep into this fight, whether he liked it or not.

Ra shook his head. "I'm fine," he promised.

"Are you sure? It can't have been easy for you to do this." Frey eyed the hand on the floor. "I'm sorry he left."

Ra opened his arms, and Frey pressed between them, relieved that Ra wasn't pushing him away. There might not be much he could do in the fight against Apophis and Maahes, but he *could* be there for Ra. He suspected Ra would need him. It couldn't be easy to find out one of his own had betrayed him and everything he believed in.

It was useless to go after Maahes. There was no way for anyone to know where he'd gone, so Ra didn't even try. Being a god had its perks and its downsides, like being unable to follow an enemy when they ran, because they could go anywhere they wished.

At least he knew who was involved now. That wouldn't help them find Maahes, but they'd be able to stop searching for Apophis's ally and focus on what they knew about the minor god. Ra had no doubt that Apophis had made Maahes promises he had no intention of keeping. Maahes would realize that eventually, but for now, it seemed he was firmly on Apophis's side.

"What now?" Frey asked from between Ra's arms.

Ra looked down at him. "We continue searching for Maahes and trying to stop him. For now, Apophis is safely locked in the underworld." But Ra suspected that eventually, Apophis would find a way out. What would happen then? Would he be able to fight off the giant serpent, or would Apophis win this time?

Ra couldn't think like that. He had to believe that this time, too, he'd be victorious and would finally be able to live the life he'd never imagined he could have. He wanted nothing more than to spend the next hundreds of years with Frey, explore the human world, and discover what he'd been missing since he retired.

"We'll fight him," Frey promised.

Ra looked down at him. "This isn't your fight. You don't have to be here if you'd rather avoid violence and possible death."

Frey shook his head. "You're not getting rid of me that easily. I don't care if you believe my place isn't here. We're together, which means we'll fight this together, too. I might not be powerful, but it doesn't mean I'm useless."

"I never said you were useless. I just don't want anything to happen to you."

"I'll be fine."

Ra prayed they all would be. He couldn't imagine a future without Frey in it, but to have what he dreamed of, he'd have to take care of Apophis first. He stood to lose many things, friends, and people he'd come to care for.

But he couldn't stay away from this fight. Apophis

wouldn't allow it, even if Ra was ready to try. Once again, he'd have to stand up to chaos and hatred and be strong for his pantheon, but also for the human world. He hadn't thought he'd have been strong enough to do this a second time, but now, he had Frey. He had something worth fighting for, someone he didn't want to lose.

That was Apophis's mistake. He believed Ra was still the god he'd been when they'd fought the first time, and that was who he thought he'd face. He couldn't have been more wrong.

And he'd find out soon.

CHAPTER ELEVEN

Frey looked around his old house, wondering if he'd ever be back. Now that he and Ra had permanently moved to their small home in Finland, Frey was back to pack the last of the things he'd need from his house in Asgard. This place would always be his, even though he was closing it up. He'd be leaving behind most of the furniture, but his personal things were all coming with him. He was more than ready for a fresh start, even with the danger of Apophis still hovering over them. Eventually, the snake would strike, rising from the underworld. In the meantime, Frey and Ra would do their best to live their life.

"I'm going to miss you," Frey's sister said.

She was helping him and, at the same time, protecting him in case Odin came around. Frey hadn't been back since the confrontation when he and Ra had come to talk to Forseti, but Frey suspected Odin wouldn't stay silent forever. It would be the worst outcome if he started a war while Apophis was also trying to kill Ra, but it wasn't something Frey could help prevent. Whatever Odin did and whenever he did it, they'd have to deal with it then.

"You can always visit," he told Freya. "Or you could move to the human world, too."

"Maybe I will. I think I'll stick around for a while longer, though. I want to keep an eye on Odin and Thor. Are you sure you want to do this?"

Frey nodded. "Even more than I was before."

"Is it because of Ra?"

Frey had never kept secrets from his sister, so she knew that he and Ra were together. Frey suspected that she would have known even if he hadn't told her anything. It was obvious that the two of them were in love from how they behaved, or at least he believed so. "Only in part."

Freya arched a brow. "And is that part located in your pants?"

Frey made a strangled sound and pushed her. She laughed, then hooked an arm around Frey's neck and pulled him close. She pressed their foreheads together, and Frey held his breath.

He and his sister had always been close. It was hard not to have her next door, but he was getting used to it. He had Ra to distract him, but the same couldn't be said for Freya, and he couldn't help but worry about her and how she'd deal with being on her own here in Asgard.

"Go out there and be happy," she murmured. "I can see you're worrying about me, but I don't need you to be. I'll be fine."

"Odin might try hurting you."

"Try would be the right word. He won't touch me."

Frey hoped his sister was right. "You can always come to Ra and me if you need anything. I need you to remember that."

"How could I forget? You might be leaving, but it doesn't mean we're not siblings anymore. I'll always be there for you, just like you'll always be there for me. I never doubted that, even after you told me about you and Ra and that you were permanently moving to the human world. I've always wanted you to be happy, and I can see that you are."

Sometimes Frey felt guilty about how happy he was. Thankfully, the extreme weather in the human world had stopped, and there hadn't been any more natural disasters. The humans were still dealing with everything that had happened, and Apophis and Maahes were still out there. How could Frey be happy when he knew all of that?

But life with Ra was nothing like what Frey had imagined he'd have when he'd moved to Finland. He was happier than he'd ever been, happier than he *thought* he could be.

Freya patted Frey's cheek and leaned back. "Now go. Be happy for both of us. Keep an eye open for the bad guys, and let me know if they strike. I'll be by your side, fighting them alongside you and Ra."

"As long as you promise to let me know if you need anything."

"I already did, didn't I? Stop letting your doubts keep you back. Ra is waiting for you, and you're waiting for happiness. Take it and cling to it with both hands. You're lucky to have found everything you found down there."

She was right, and he couldn't wait to go back to Ra. After one last hug, he grabbed the last of his bags and returned home.

He appeared in front of the house he and Ra shared. There was snow everywhere, and it was cold and dark, but Frey loved it because he could see the light coming from inside the house. The windows in the living room were illuminated, and he could see Ra puttering around through them. The smell of food cooking reached his nose, and he winced, wondering if Ra had managed to make something edible this time around. They didn't have to eat to survive, but they felt hunger just like humans, and Frey enjoyed human food. Ra had found something he loved in cooking, but he wasn't always great at it, and he tended to experiment more than Frey was comfortable with.

But whatever Ra had cooked, he'd eat it. He never wanted Ra to feel like he shouldn't do something or like he might need to go back to isolating himself. He was still learning about the human world and having fun with it. Who was Frey to tell him not to do something?

This was his future. He was home and loved this place more than he'd ever loved Asgard. He'd fight to the death to defend it from Odin, Apophis, or anyone else who'd try to take it from him.

Ra had discovered the joys of human music, and he enjoyed listening to it as he cooked dinner for Frey. Frey should be back soon, and Ra couldn't wait.

He was always nervous when Frey was out of sight, but he was trying to fix that. It was terrifying to him that Apophis might decide to hurt Frey just to hurt *him*, but he wouldn't put it past the serpent. Hopefully, Maahes hadn't realized how important Frey was to Ra. Frey had stayed away from Ra during the meeting. As far as Ra knew, Maahes hadn't talked to anyone else.

The fact that Ra was in a relationship with a god from another pantheon wasn't a secret. Most of the gods in his pantheon had stayed away from him and didn't bother telling him what they thought of it, so he hoped no one had babbled to Maahes. If they had, though, he doubted they'd let him know. He didn't think anyone would have done so on purpose to make him more vulnerable, but that was what would happen. If Maahes and Apophis found out how important Frey was to Ra, they'd try to strike Ra through him, and that wasn't something Ra was ready to deal with. He didn't think he would *ever* be ready to. Frey was his life — a life he hadn't thought he'd have.

After retiring, he'd believed the rest of his immortal life would be spent in his wing of the palace on his own, with a few visits from his parent and the closest of his friends. Instead, he was living in the human world, in love with Frey, and about to face another battle with Apophis.

This was nothing like he'd expected, but he loved it. He couldn't wait for Apophis to be gone, because then he'd be able to focus on Frey and their future.

The sound of the front door opening made him turn. No one had visited them since they'd moved here, so it could only be Frey. Ra found himself smiling before Frey even appeared, and his smile widened when Frey did.

He was wearing a light jacket, a pair of jeans, and socks on his feet. He'd no doubt left his boots by the front door.

"You cooked," he said.

"I hope you don't mind." Ra wasn't an idiot and knew that Frey didn't always love what he cooked. It was fine with him. He liked experimenting, and Frey was never mean about it. "Nothing elaborate tonight," Ra said as he strode toward Frey. "Just some pasta."

Frey relaxed. "That's good. I like pasta."

"Is there anyone who doesn't?"

"I'm sure there is. I'll never be in that camp, though."

"Then I'll cook a lot of pasta for you." Ra leaned down, pushed Frey's jacket from his shoulders, and kissed him as he slid it off his arms. Frey relaxed against him, sighing happily.

Ra still had a hard time believing he could make someone happy, but he had no doubt that was how Frey felt with him. He never wanted to lose that, which was what would happen if Apophis won, but that wasn't something Ra was willing to consider, tonight or any other night. Right now, he wanted to focus on Frey and the happiness they shared.

"How did it go?" he asked as he dropped Frey's jacket on the back of one of the chairs at the table.

"I didn't have any trouble, if that's what you're asking."

"Well, it was a worry of mine, but it's good to know that Odin didn't try to stop you."

"He doesn't care about me."

"He seemed angry back when I was in Asgard."

"That's because he's always angry. He doesn't care about me, though, so I wouldn't worry if I were you."

"How can I not worry? He's powerful."

"He is, and he likes that power. He wants to be in control, which is why he was so pissed when we approached Forseti. That's who he cares about. Not me."

Ra wasn't sure about that. Even if Odin didn't care about Frey, he cared about appearances and about the fact that Frey had defied him.

But those were worries for another day.

He forced himself to forget about Odin and focus on Frey. "Come sit down. I don't want the food to get cold."

Frey looked exhausted, even though he'd only been to Asgard to finish packing his things. Probably it had been emotionally hard more than physically, which was understandable. No matter how unhappy Frey had been in Asgard, it was all he'd known for thousands of years. And no matter how happy Frey was now, it was still an adjustment to live in the human world and share his home and life with another god, especially one like Ra. Ra was very much aware of the fact that he wasn't an easy person to get along with. But Frey was ready to try, and that was all that mattered in the end.

Ra lowered the volume of the radio before grabbing two plates and filling them. The table was already set, so the only thing left for them to do was to sit down and eat.

Frey gave him a tired smile when Ra placed a plate in front of him. Ra hadn't been lying when he'd said he'd kept it simple. It was just pasta with a pesto sauce, something he'd discovered recently. He liked making his own pesto, and luckily, with his powers, it was easy to find a big supply of basil. The smells rising from his plate were tantalizing, so he grabbed his fork, ready to dig in.

"This is lovely," Frey said after swallowing his first bite. He sounded relieved.

Ra wasn't offended. He'd tasted everything he'd cooked, and sometime, it was a disaster. He didn't need Frey to tell him that.

"How was your day?" Frey asked.

It hit Ra once again that he wouldn't have had this if he'd stayed in retirement. When he'd decided to leave life behind, he'd thought it was the best thing for him and everyone else. He'd believed he'd be happy, staying away from trouble and focusing on himself. Maybe he had been for a time, but it hadn't lasted long. He'd needed more to life, and now, he had it.

And he'd do whatever he had to protect it. He'd fight Apophis to death this time if that was what he needed to do to keep Frey and the rest of their family alive.

Because that was what Loki and the others were. Ra had never been close to other gods the way he was to them and Frey, and he wasn't ready to lose them, especially not to Apophis. Soon, it would be time for them to take a stance and fight the serpent. Even though the natural disasters had slowed down, Frey and Ra agreed on the fact that Apophis was just biding his time. He'd strike, and they'd have to be ready for him when he did.

Ra wasn't sure they would be. He didn't think anyone could ever be ready for Apophis and the chaos and pain he'd unleash on the human world and anyone who stood up to him.

But Ra had many more things to fight for now. He had *people* to fight for, and those people would fight with him. That wasn't something he'd had before.

He looked up at Frey and grabbed his free hand, squeezing it.

No matter how deep the darkness rising against them was, they'd fight it and bring the light back. Ra wouldn't have it any other way.

EPILOGUE

"Are these meetings necessary?" Jimmy grumbled. "I mean, no offense because I love all of you, but I'd rather talk about something that isn't the end of the world every time we see each other."

Ra smiled. He hadn't known what to make of Jimmy for a long time. More often than not, he still didn't. He found the human odd, but Jimmy had welcomed him into his life, and Ra hadn't pulled away from that.

He looked around the office. He hadn't pulled away from any of the people here today, even though he'd been tempted many times. Sometimes, it was just too much for him to be with so many people. Other times, he worried he was putting them in danger. They were all adults, and they all knew what they stood to lose if something happened. They knew that Apophis was lurking in the underworld, plotting their demise.

Yet, they were here anyway.

Ra swallowed and leaned harder against Frey's chest. Frey looked down and tightened the arm he had around Ra's shoulders, pulling him even closer. "Everything okay?" he murmured.

Ra nodded. "I'm just not sure what to do."

"Which is why we're here," Loki said from Ra's other side. He was cradling his son, cooing at him as he listened to the conversations in the room.

They always gathered in the human palace in Egypt. Ra wasn't sure why, although maybe it was to make things easier on the humans. Sam traveled with Loki, but Jimmy and Mery were already there. It was their home and the place where Mery needed to be. As a pharaoh, he had to be able to step in if anything happened, and that was easier if he was in his palace. Everyone else could easily travel back and forth, and they did.

"I'll get someone to bring us food," Jimmy declared. "It'll make for a cheerier meeting."

"There's nothing cheery about a massive snake wanting to kill us all," Sam pointed out.

Sam was the most vocally pessimistic of them. Ra was even more pessimistic, but he didn't often voice his doubts. He was the only one who knew how dangerous Apophis truly was, and he didn't want to scare his family. He doubted they'd decide not to help even if he did, but he wasn't ready to bet on that, and more importantly, he didn't want to freak them out before he had to. They deserved to live and be happy without waiting until Apophis made his next move.

"Do we know anything new?" Mery asked. He was always logical and calm, for which Ra was grateful.

They all looked at Ra, waiting for him to answer. He shook his head and sat up straighter. "As you're all aware, the number of natural disasters and extreme weather episodes has gone down drastically. It's clear that Apophis either isn't able to sustain them anymore, or that he decided to stop for some reason."

"That's what worries me," Sam muttered.

Ra nodded. "I have to admit I'm worried, too. I'm hoping this is happening because Apophis isn't strong enough, but I'm afraid to believe that. Knowing him, he's just taking a break and plotting his next move."

"What about Maahes? Has anyone seen him?"

"There have been a few sightings, but every time we think we've got him, he's gone by the time we reach the place where he was seen. From what we've been able to gather, he's always on the move, which might mean he's unable to raise more demons for Apophis to use."

"And that's why there hasn't been any catastrophic episodes again?"

"Unfortunately, I know as much as you do when it comes to that."

Sam slowly nodded, then turned his attention to Frey. "What about your visions?"

Frey had told everyone about the visions and informed them every time he had one. Ra stayed by his side through all of them, making sure he was okay once they were over. Frey had explained he'd had visions for his entire life, that he was used to them and that Ra didn't need to hover, but Ra wasn't willing to risk it.

"Unfortunately, they haven't been telling me anything new," Frey explained. "It's just the same old giant snake coming toward me in a world of darkness. I still have no idea what the darkness means, although Ra thinks it could be the underworld."

Sam frowned. "Is that how the underworld is? Just a giant expense of darkness?"

"I've never been there," Ra said. "Not many gods have. Osiris is our representative, along with a few others, and he takes care of everything. The underworld is his domain, as it should be."

"I get that, but it would be easier if we could find out exactly where Apophis is. We wouldn't have to wait for him to come to us. We could go to him and kill him."

Ra knew that this time around, he'd have to kill Apophis to make him stop. He'd gotten away with just dropping him in the underworld last time, but it wasn't a long-term solution, clearly. Ra didn't want to deal with Apophis again every few thousand years.

"I'm planning on meeting with Osiris next week," Ra explained. "Hopefully, he can give me more details about what's been happening. He doesn't know Apophis's exact location, but he has a much better idea of what's happening in the underworld. I'm sure that now that Apophis isn't focused on the human world, the underworld is feeling his anger."

"You'll tell us what you find out?" Loki asked.

"Like always." Ra sucked in a breath. "I know this isn't the best scenario. No matter how hard everyone works, we're not anywhere close to finding Apophis or Maahes. That means that at the moment, we have to wait for them to come to us, which puts us in more danger than if we could go to them. I promise I'm doing everything I can to locate both of them."

Loki patted Ra's knee. "We know you are. No one blames you for what's happening. Besides, they're giving us some reprieve. I think we should all take advantage of that, because the fight ahead of us isn't going to be easy."

Ra agreed. He leaned back against Frey, letting his lover hold his weight. The fight would be messy and bloody, and Ra might lose someone who was in the room with him right now. Their family wouldn't be standing against Apophis alone, though. More and more gods were coming to Ra, telling him they wanted to help. Maybe soon, they'd be an army facing off against Apophis and Maahes, and Ra was confident they could win.

They had to.

ABOUT THE AUTHOR

Catherine is the creator of several series, most of them paranormal, including the Whitedell Pride Series and the Gillham Pack Series. While she graduated in translation, she decided to go the writer's way because it was more fun to create her own stories and characters.

She's been living in Italy for more than twenty years, but she's a daughter of the North—Belgium to be precise—and she misses it so much that she's already planning to move back.

She loves pizza—probably too much—her son, her pets, and of course, books. She sneaks some reading time into her schedule every time she has five minutes free from writing, demands from her various pets and son, and lastly, housework.

Connect with her:

lievens.catherine@gmail.com
BookBub: https://www.bookbub.com/authors/catherine-lievens
Website: https://authorcatherinelievens.com/
Facebook: https://www.facebook.com/catherine.lievens.9
Facebook   Group: https://www.facebook.com/groups/411788002341528/
Twitter: https://twitter.com/authorCLievens
Newsletter: http://eepurl.com/c-uvKn